PRAISE FOR **On the**

Winner of the Nordic

"What the best novels can do is open up spaces. Balle has opened a space in time, and it is absolutely, absolutely incredible. What a fantastic book." —Karl Ove Knausgård

"A masterpiece of its time" —Nordic Council Literature Prize

★ "The richly strange first book of the Danish author Balle's seven-part novel is a dreamy, quirky, and indefinitely prolonged version of *Groundhog Day*. The philosophical conundrum at the novel's heart is grounded in the ordinariness of everyday domestic life, and the dilemmas of a marriage in which one partner changes and the other doesn't. A cliffhanger will leave readers anxious to read book two." —*Booklist* (starred)

"A steady, careful, and deeply disquieting estrangement of a single day ... it is impossible to put down." —Kate Briggs

"Solvej Balle is a prodigious writer who, miraculously, finds the subtlest, most fascinating differences in repetition. You have never read anything like *On the Calculation of Volume*. This unforgettable novel is a profound meditation on the lonely, untranslatable ways in which each one of us inhabits time—and the tenuous yet indelible traces we leave in the world. Day after day." —Hernan Diaz

"An unparalleled cliffhanger." —*Morgenbladet*

"A new, original, and brilliantly beautiful book. Reading it is like being caressed by language itself. The novel's plan is accomplished with relentless consequence, concise uncanniness, and its own dry intensity." —*Information*

"A crazy, philosophical, and addictive novel." —*Les Inrockuptibles*

"A superb reflection on solitude, individual responsibility, existential fatigue, and the fear of losing those we love. It is a study of the setbacks, shifts, and illusions that we weave against the flow of time." —*Libération*

"A total explosion: Solvej Balle has blown through to a new dimension of literary exploration." —Nicole Krauss

"Existential questions about the core and functioning of human relationships are raised here in a virtuosic and seemingly incidental manner. *On the Calculation of Volume* is a dazzling, poetic, tremendously multi-layered novel. Temporal anomalies and great literature have never been so successfully combined. Fascinating, extraordinary." —*Horazio* (Germany)

"A hypnotic feat of prose writing." —John Vincler, *Cultured*

"A meticulous narration, during which monotony and repetition seem to be an integral part of the aesthetic project. If the idea of making literary characters exist in different temporalities is not new, its implementation is undoubtedly new here." —*Le Monde*

ON THE
CALCULATION
OF VOLUME

II

SOLVEJ BALLE

on the calculation
of volume

II

*translated from the Danish
by Barbara J. Haveland*

A NEW DIRECTIONS
PAPERBOOK ORIGINAL

Published by arrangement with Copenhagen Literary Agency
Originally published by Pelagraf as *Om udregning af rumfang II* in 2020

Manufactured in the United States of America
First published in 2024 as New Directions Paperbook 1676
(ISBN 978-0-8112-3727-7)
Design by Erik Rieselbach

Library of Congress Cataloging-in-Publication Data
Names: Balle, Solvej, 1962– author. | Haveland, Barbara, translator.
Title: On the calculation of volume / Solvej Balle ;
translated from the Danish by Barbara J. Haveland.
Other titles: Om udregning af rumfang. English
Description: New York : New Directions Publishing, 2024.
Identifiers: LCCN 2024032043 | ISBN 9780811237253 (v. 1 ; paperback) |
ISBN 9780811237260 (v. 1 ; ebook)
Subjects: LCGFT: Science fiction. | Novels.
Classification: LCC PT8176.12.A384 0413 2024 |
DDC 839.813/74—dc23/eng/20240711
LC record available at https://lccn.loc.gov/2024032043

2 4 6 8 10 9 7 5 3 1

New Directions Books are published for James Laughlin
by New Directions Publishing Corporation
80 Eighth Avenue, New York 10011

ON THE
CALCULATION
OF VOLUME

II

#368

What had I imagined? Time as a carousel one could jump on
and off? The year as a stream running underneath my eighteenth of November?

I'm sitting by the window in Room 16 of the Hôtel du Lison.
I have accumulated days. 365 November days. But what good
does it do? As if a pile of identical autumn days constituted a
year. And what good does it do to wander around at the end
of the year poised to leap? Or dive? A year of waiting, then the
eighteenth of November would come around again and I would
be able to escape from the circle of repetition at the point where
I entered? Was that what I had imagined: an eighteenth of November with open doors and free passage to recognizable time?
Perhaps. But that is not how it works.

I wander around in my eighteenth of November. I have been
looking for a way out, but there is no way out. I have been
searching for differences, but there are no differences. It is the
same day and now I don't know how I could have thought that
underneath all my days there lay a normal year with a new eighteenth of November slowly approaching. As if a truer chronology were to be found somewhere down there in the depths, as
if all my repetitions were just the surface and the real year had
sought shelter under a succession of eighteenths of November
As if a new eighteenth of November would rise up at the end
of the year and take me back. Or pass by, allowing me to jump
on while it was moving, out of my maelstrom of repetitions.

As if a plank would come floating by, a different eighteenth of November, to rescue me from my sea of repetitions, a piece of driftwood I could grab and cling to until I reached solid ground, until I was tossed ashore on a nineteenth of November, on a day with a fresh newspaper to read with my coffee, a different receptionist at the desk, a morning with no rain. Or with pouring rain, flooding, thunder, snow, anything, as long as it was different. As if my 365th day represented a magical ending, not just one in an endless run of numbers. As if my 366th day marked a new beginning, a new eighteenth of November. Allowing passage to the nineteenth. And the twentieth. As if there were a way out, not just a day that passed only to make way for the next eighteenth of November and the next again, for day 367 and day 368 and, tomorrow, day 369.

If nothing happened the run of numbers would never end. Nothing has happened and the run of numbers never ends. No new and different eighteenth of November came around, no truer chronology bubbled up from the depths, no lifesaving plank came floating past, I have not been tossed ashore on the nineteenth of November and there is no change in sight.

Yesterday I woke up early. I had fallen into a deep sleep after returning to the hotel, exhausted after my days in suspense, waiting for a new and altered November day. I woke with a start and was immediately aware of the box containing the Roman sestertius which Philip Maurel had given me. It lay in its bag next to my pillow and I remembered what had happened: how I had met Philip and gone back to his shop with him. How Philip and Marie had shown me their new apartment. I remembered our wander through the former resident's belongings. I had told them everything: how time had fallen apart, how I hoped to return to a recognizable time. They had sent me away with a Roman sestertius in a bag.

I got up straight away, dressed and went down to the reception desk. I had no idea what time it was, but the newspapers were already laid out and they were the same newspapers. From the eighteenth. Fresh and untouched. In the breakfast room the coffee was starting to run through the machine, the tables were set and the staff were busy putting bread and croissants on platters and in baskets. I took a seat, hoping that something would be different from on all the other November days, but there was no difference and soon I saw the morning repeat itself. I saw familiar faces and gestures. I saw a slice of bread fall to the floor, a gentle, drifting descent. It was the eighteenth yet again. Of course it was.

All day, from the moment I woke until I went to bed that night, everything was exactly the same as on all the other days, a day full of recognition, and when I woke this morning it was the eighteenth once again. There is no difference. I have passed unhindered into Year 2, or rather: I have reached the eighteenth of November number 368 in a time without years, without seasons, a time without weeks or months, with nothing but a single day that keeps recurring, and I can only imagine that it will continue to do so. I cannot imagine anything else. It is a fault that cannot be remedied. It is now chronic. The only thing that comes around again is my day. There is morning and there is evening and there is night and there is morning again—same day.

I sit in Room 16 of the Hôtel du Lison. Today I did not have breakfast. I got no further than reception, glanced at the newspapers then turned on my heel and went back to my room. I do not want to see slices of bread drifting floorward.

#369

Today I was awake long before it was light. I was woken by the corner of the sestertius's box digging into my cheek. It was still in its bag next to my pillow, I must have rolled onto it in my sleep, but now I am awake, I am up, I am out in the morning gloom and it is still the eighteenth. It has not turned into the nineteenth, it has not turned into the twentieth and it has not turned into the twenty-first and why would it?

It was far too early to get up, but I got dressed all the same. I pulled on my boots, I buttoned my coat, picked my bag up off the floor and before leaving the room I took the box with the sestertius out of the bag on the bed, removed the coin from the box, slipped it into my pocket and left the box and the bag on the table. I took my key with me, there was no one at the reception desk, and I went out to walk through the almost deserted streets in the darkness.

I returned to the hotel a couple of hours later, just after seven, by which time it was light. I helped myself to a cup of coffee from the buffet and brought it up here, and now I am sitting at the little table in my room. I know that the eighteenth of November will continue, I don't know what to do about the day, but now I know what I can expect. Eighteenths of November, that is what I can expect.

#374

Every day I visit my streets. I cross the boulevard Chaminade and walk along the passage du Cirque. I cut across the little square at the top of the rue Renart and carry on down the rue Almageste. I sit in a café or on a park bench.

Nothing has changed and there is nothing I have to do. There are no books to be bought, no auctions to attend, no friends to visit. I have no pattern of sounds and silence around which to organize my day, I have no plans, I have no calendar. Time passes, but all it does is pour day after day into my world, it goes nowhere, it has no stops or stations, only this endless chain of days.

I pass the antiquarian bookshops in the area, but I don't go in. I look at the books in the windows, waver briefly, then walk on. I make my circles bigger and find other streets. In the rue d'Ésope I stopped outside a bookshop I didn't know. I felt like going in to take a closer look at a couple of the works in the window, but I stayed outside. I have no business in there, they are the bookshops of the past and I am no longer T. & T. Selter.

I have come by Philip Maurel's shop and once or twice I have stopped by the window and peered down into the shop. I only do this when Marie is on her own in there, I don't want to be recognized, I know when Philip comes and goes and I don't want to meet him.

I still have the sestertius. It's in my coat pocket and Marie has put another coin on display on the counter. Last night when I went to bed I forgot to take the coin out of my pocket and put it under my pillow, but when I woke this morning it was still there. I can feel it as I roam the streets. If I had a dog I could say that I was walking the dog. Now I am walking a Roman coin. An odd companion.

It is noticeable in the streets. An emptiness. As if something has disappeared. I feel it in the grit on the rue Desterres and when I hurry across the rue Almageste. A condensed mass that has dissolved. There are fewer details now. It feels concrete, almost physical, as if the traffic has thinned out, or the pedestrians are gone, as if the light and the sounds have changed, as if the gaps between the buildings have grown, the streets have widened, but I know that nothing has changed, there are still people around, there is still traffic, neither the light nor the sounds have changed. It is simply that I no longer have any business here. I walk the same streets, but borne along purely by routine and old habit. In the past I have always had good reason to be here, but now I feel superfluous. I walk around the city with no purpose other than my own passage from day to day. I am merely a human being roaming the streets, or maybe not even a human being, maybe more of an animal of some sort, neither hunter nor hunted, neither hungry nor well-fed, just a creature wandering up and down.

#378

I woke up late today and it was afternoon before I went out. I took a different route from the one I usually take, but again I was struck by that feeling, a sort of emptiness, a sense of something missing.

As I roamed the streets I began to feel dizzy. I was shivering and I looked around for somewhere to go, off the street, but there seemed to be no room anywhere. There were no obvious spots, nowhere to which I could retreat, where I could just sit down for a while. I glanced about for a park or a bench, but there was no space for me. The places I usually frequent seemed shuttered and unapproachable. None of the benches or café chairs I could see were for me. No sidewalk or pedestrian crossing matched my steps. I felt out of place, a foreign body. I did not belong and there was nothing I could do about it.

In the end I went into an almost empty café where I tried to sit down at a window table, but the chairs felt as though they were trying to shake me off. At first it was just the one chair which seemed a little unsteady under me, so I got up and fetched another one and sat down, but then there appeared to be something wrong with the table. I shifted it slightly and moved the chair about a bit. I felt confused and alarmed and when I finally managed to steady the furniture there was no one to take my order, so I left the café and went back to the streets.

It made no difference. The streets felt deserted. The atmosphere seemed to have changed, the air was thinner, as if a substance had leached out of the asphalt, rendering it porous, or maybe it was a subtle change in the color of the buildings, I don't know. Something was gone, something to do with the colors, or maybe the sounds, as if one of the world's elements had suddenly drained away, or perhaps it was more like a new kind of emptiness, an unknown strain.

I tried to walk off this feeling on my way through the streets. I turned corners and found busy streets and bustling arcades and gradually the world began to look more like itself. I made it to shore, back to the world and spent most of the afternoon walking around, trying to steer clear of this feeling of emptiness. I walked through parks, along gravel paths, past benches and playgrounds, not sitting down anywhere, except for a few minutes when I attempted to sit on a slightly damp bench beside the fountain in the passage du Cirque.

Late in the afternoon I returned to the hotel, bought a sandwich at the reception desk and went up to my room. On my way up the stairs I glanced down at myself with a feeling that there was something rather worn about my appearance: something ragged, scruffy, something frayed, but I couldn't figure out what it was. I looked in a mirror as I turned down the corridor leading to my room. It was not my clothes, they were no shabbier than when I was last here, I had worn the same boots on many of my trips out of the spare room in Clairon, but they were not particularly battered looking. I was wearing a dress, a different one from the last time I was here, I had left the old one in Clairon, this one was newer, there was nothing wrong with it, and my coat looked the same as always. I could possibly do with a new one, but it's not that noticeable. And yet I had the air of having been stowed away in an attic: threadbare, dusty and out of circulation.

I know, of course, that it is just me: that I have lost my way. There is no missing element. There is no newly discovered strain of emptiness. I simply cannot find any reason for making my way through the streets. I walk past shops and have no urge to enter them. I cross a street or stroll through a park and I feel out of sorts, superfluous, bedraggled, wrong. I am no longer Tara Selter, antiquarian bookseller with an eye for detail and an instinct for collectable works. I am not Tara Selter at work. I am not a buyer for a company by the name of T. & T. Selter. She is no more: the Tara Selter who goes in to inquire, deal, inspect, purchase, agree, organize. It is the Tara Selter, antiquarian bookseller, who is gone, a person at work, with a business that is growing, flourishing, a dealer with customers and colleagues. It is the Tara Selter with a future who is gone. It is the Tara Selter with hopes and dreams who has fallen out of the picture, been thrown off the world, run over the edge, been poured out, carried off down the stream of eighteenths of November, lost, evaporated, swept out to sea.

Back in my room I put my sandwich on the table and took off my coat and boots, but shortly afterward, as I was attempting to eat this somewhat dry offering, the hotel fire alarm went off. This surprised me for a moment because I had never heard the alarm go off before, but that had to be because I had not been at the hotel just after five o'clock on any other day. The alarm did not worry me because the hotel had not burned down and I had never seen any sign of a fire, so I stayed where I was and moments later the alarm stopped. I got up and went to the window.

There were people out on the street. So, I thought, the eighteenth of November also contains a false alarm at the Hôtel du Lison. So what? I thought. So nothing. I saw a fire truck drive up, but there was no sign of a fire and the hose was not rolled out. A fireman was chatting quietly with the hotel receptionist and I sat down again and took another bite of my sandwich.

Only afterward did I realize what that meant: that I was no longer on my guard, that I am no longer looking for lifesaving planks, that I never even considered the possibility that the Hôtel du Lison might be on fire, that this could have been a different eighteenth of November, that this could have been a leap into a new time, that the hotel could have been about to burn down and that I could have been in danger at the very moment when time leapt back into its normal course. I simply assumed that it was a false alarm.

A few days ago I would have jumped to my feet, scenting change, but I just sat there with my half-eaten sandwich and did nothing and the sandwich is still lying here on the table next to me, not because it was left in haste due to an evacuation, but because it is a bit dry around the edges. I no longer believe in variation, I don't look for differences and not even a fire alarm can alter my expectations of a day that comes around again and again.

I can still hear voices in the corridors outside my door, but the sidewalk across the road from the hotel was clear of people a while ago. The last hotel guests are making their way back to their rooms, the fire engine soon left the scene again and there is no danger. It is a quiet day at the Hôtel du Lison. No one has been hurt, no one has been injured. I sit in my hotel room, I am safe, Thomas is safe in his eighteenth of November in Clairon, he got drenched by the rain and has come back to a house that has grown chilly, but nothing else has happened. He is back in his living room, he has lit a fire, he has fetched a leek from the garden and some onions from the garden shed. There is no cause for concern. I have a husband who thinks I have a better chance of finding a solution on my own. I have friends who do not think they can help and who may not even believe I am telling the truth, but who sent me away with a Roman sestertius in a bag. Tara Selter's final mission: up the steps and out with her garbage bag. And now I am walking around the streets, superfluous and out of circulation. It is not a disaster. It is not nothing, but it is not much either.

#379

And now, when the eighteenth of November has become chronic: my days are simple, I frequent familiar streets, but I don't belong there. I hear footsteps at my back. I grow anxious. I look around. I get it into my head that there is someone who wants something of me and that what they want of me is not good. But there is no one behind me, it is my own footsteps I hear and even the sound of my own feet is superfluous. I am walking through a space that ought to be empty. The place I occupy ought to be vacant, but for some inexplicable reason Tara Selter has taken it.

All around me people are going to work. They are opening shops and heading for metro stations. They move in formations, they take directions, they are pulled along, but I don't feel that same pull, it is a cord I lack, this is something I am not a part of. I cannot catch hold. Either that or it is something that washes them along the streets, a current that carries them along, but this current cannot reach me. Or perhaps it is some inner mechanism. Something that steers their feet through the streets, an inner drive which I don't possess, a spring that cannot be tightened, a mechanism that is missing. I don't know whether they are being pulled, carried along by the current or whether inner mechanisms are propelling them along the streets, but I know that, whatever it is, it doesn't work on me.

I am surrounded by people in motion. Suddenly they are all walking in the same direction. I look around me and, sure enough, there is a metro station and that is where they are headed. There are lines of people pointing towards the way down. I am outside of the lines. If I get too close to their lines I am in the way. I am a foreign body, an error. I am Tara Selter, lost in the eighteenth of November. Not lost and forsaken, just lost. I have fallen out of the day, but this is not tragic, this is not comic, I have simply fallen out of the world, I have not been hurt in the fall, I got up and brushed a little grit off my knee, that is all.

My name is Tara Selter. I find myself in the eighteenth of November, there is an echo around me. I am a strange creature that ought not to be among people with a direction. That ought to be moving on. That gets in the way of people trying to tend to their business.

I edge out of the hectic lines, I step aside. I discover streets I do not know, I turn unfamiliar corners, I come upon cafés I have never visited before. I carry my echo with me, there is a distinctly hollow ring to the sound when I pull out the chair at a table in the corner and sit down. I place my bag on the chair next to me. The bag is large enough to give me the appearance of a traveler but small enough for me to have it with me during the day. It makes me look as though I have business I ought to be tending to, but I am still in the way, though occasionally I find a corner of the world where I can sit for a moment. I breathe. I stay calm.

I can count my days and I do. I can write about them and I do. I have a small notebook containing strokes and numbers. I have a folder full of notes from the eighteenth of November, I have money and credit cards. I have a pen with the inscription *7ème Salon Lumières*, I can write whatever I please, I can go wherever I please, I want for nothing.

I walk along the edge of a precipice, I count days and make notes. I do it in order to remember. Or I do it in order to hold the days together. Or perhaps I do it because the paper remembers what I say. As if I existed. As if someone were listening.

#383

I had thought I would go back. To Clairon-sous-Bois. To Thomas. If nothing happened. If a year meant nothing. If there was no way out at the end of the year. Maybe I would visit Philip and Marie first. I imagine that I would have asked their advice, that we would have sat around the counter and they would have suggested various solutions, each one weirder than the one before. That we would have found the situation funny. There should have been laughter. We should have talked about dust and burns while laughing at the quirks of time. I imagined, I suppose, that they would be able to help me, that they would try, that they would pretend to be trying. That they would at least laugh. And if there wasn't a way out, I would probably take the train back to Clairon. I would walk through the rain, I would tell Thomas that I had returned because time had ground to a halt, that I had tried to jump back, that I had been poised to leap, that that was what I wanted: to go back. To Thomas, to Philip and Marie, to the people on the street, to currents and lines, to the common rhythm, to Tara Selter, antiquarian book-seller with a feel for paper and an eye for detail. That it wasn't that I didn't want to go by their time. But that there was nothing I could do. I had tried.

But maybe I am simply alone. Maybe I do not belong. Maybe it cannot be any other way. I do try, though. I gather myself and sometimes when I enter a stream of people on the street, if I come past a bus stop just as a bus pulls up and am suddenly caught up in a group of people waiting to board and if I follow the stream onto the bus, or if I approach from the right direction and am walking at the right speed past a metro station, my rhythm will suddenly fit, I am in step, sometimes I am almost carried along, I climb on and off, I am steered, it is almost like being understood, like being given advice. If one listens.

Usually it doesn't last long, because when the bus suddenly empties again and I follow the stream onto the sidewalk, or when I emerge onto the street at an unfamiliar spot, I am once more alone. The stream of people disperses, the sound of my footsteps on the sidewalk, which had been lost in the crowd, rings out again and the echoes around me can be heard once more. The street opens out, the mass of people who helped me along had a goal, one that I borrowed for a moment, but now here I am, the people have dispersed, have fanned out and boarded other forms of transport, have poured into buildings or hurried off down other streets, and I too walk off, although not as briskly, I slacken my pace, I saunter through the streets and sooner or later I find myself back at the Hôtel du Lison.

Nonetheless, I go out again the following day. I pack my bag, I roam around in the emptiness, but I am ready to follow if someone should show the way and then, if I should suddenly find myself caught up in a movement, a stream, if I feel a pull, a direction, I go with it. It's not very hard. You have to be ready, but then it happens quite naturally. It's like standing on a beach, the water is cold, you're ready, you want to jump in but you hold back, rooted to the spot, as if there is a barrier between you and the water, but then someone else comes running past and jumps straight in and you follow them, caught in the other person's slipstream, you push off and all at once you are in the water, you duck under, dive, swim through the cold water, ice-cold to begin with and then, suddenly, no longer cold at all. All hesitancy is gone, you were not swept along, you ran into the water all by yourself, you ducked under all by yourself, you have shouldered responsibility for your own running, diving and swimming, you no longer need to be led in any direction, you are in motion and can carry on as if you had never faltered at all

This is how I pass my days: I throw myself into the crowd, I let myself be carried along, I am in motion, I go with the current, but in the end, once I have followed the streams, once I have boarded buses and trains and stepped off them again, once I have emerged from the metro stations or landed on the sidewalk at a bus stop, I lose momentum. I slow down, stop. There seems to be something wrong with the mechanism that my motion is supposed to trigger. A spark is ignited, but I stall, slow down, pull to the side. I drive onto the hard shoulder, I cannot keep up so I head for quieter streets. And that's all right. I'm not lost, I simply find a bench where I can stop and sit down for a while, or I start to walk back, I head for the hotel and by the end of the day my pace has slowed completely, I go to bed and the next day I find fresh streams of people to throw myself into.

#387

My circles have grown bigger. One day I got as far as the Bois de Boulogne, another day I went all the way out to Fontainebleau, and now I am on a train traveling north. I have no ticket because I merely followed the stream of people and suddenly we were heading toward the train. I had been following the morning rush. At a bus stop I joined the line boarding a bus that took me to the Gare du Nord, a stream of people carried me through the station and now I am on a train to Lille. There are people on the train, they are on their way, I don't know where to or why, but we will soon be getting off because Lille-Europe is the end of the line.

My bag is on the floor beside me, it is lighter now because my books, my extra clothes and my toiletries are still at the hotel.

However, I did happen to take the key to Room 16 with me, but I won't be needing that. The key to the house in Clairon, to Thomas's house, is also in my bag. It would be easy to go back. I know the way. All of this is familiar to me. I know the stations, but it's not the right way.

#388

I got off at Lille. The early morning traffic turned into the mid-morning traffic, the streams of people thinned out, I was the last passenger to leave the train, slowly and hesitantly, so slowly that I ground to a halt on the platform. All at once there were no people around me and I was not being carried anywhere. Shortly afterward I left the station, found a hotel nearby, then went for a stroll around the city. I wanted to buy a toothbrush, but suddenly I found myself outside a stationery store where I had once bought a notebook with a green cloth binding that I never got around to using. I went inside and in the same spot as before sat a pile of notebooks with green cloth bindings. One of them had to be mine, I told myself and I bought one, possibly the same one. Possibly one that just looked like it.

Yesterday evening I put it under my pillow along with a newly purchased toothbrush and a tube of toothpaste and it is all still there. I woke early, had breakfast at the hotel and no one dropped a piece of bread, there were no morning newspapers and I don't miss them. I don't miss the things I left in Room 16, I feel lighter without my books and I can manage with the clothes I have on. My step is light, weightless, empty almost.

#389

The notebook is in my bag on the seat next to me, waiting to be used, but I have not taken it out. It just lies there with its lines while I write on paper from my folder, because I still have paper. I have my pen and my bag. I have my seat on the train, I have my coat and a phone that has once again stopped working.

Around me are people with coats and bags and phones. I can hear that some of them have lives which they are getting on with, they have places to go and things to do. I don't know if I have a life which I am getting on with, but there is nothing I have to do and nowhere I have to be. I have ears to hear, though, and if one wants one can borrow snippets from one's fellow passengers: their lives and places, the things they have to do. Or steal, because it feels as if one is taking something from them. As if one is not meant to listen. They give it away, but it doesn't really feel like a gift.

One man is busy arranging a conference or an annual meeting, there is some disagreement regarding this and he is phoning around and making his case: a new board of directors has to be elected, decisions have to be made and he is endeavoring to engender some sort of consensus or harmony, like a choirmaster who has to get the choir to harmonize without anyone realizing that he is the choirmaster. It sounds complicated, he calls one person, then another and we sit around him on the train, passengers in his choir machine, we listen in because it's impossible not to. I think it has to do with a sailing club. He talks about the purchase of boats, about attracting more young people, he wants to get the junior club membership up and running, he says. He talks about financing and sponsorship, about big plans, about a clubhouse. I don't know where he is going. We are nowhere near the sea, my curiosity has been aroused, he speaks to various people, instructing them in what they should say at the meeting. We cannot be sure of the outcome, but now I am considering following him, because the meeting is this evening, he will just make it before it starts, he says.

He's on his way to Dunkirk. So he tells the conductor. He has to change trains soon and I feel like going to the seaside. I feel like sailing, feel like traveling on ferries or sailboats, to water, to a horizon.

But then he puts down his phone and now he is on his computer, the wind goes out of his sails, they flap a little, then my attention turns: I can hear a woman arranging dinner with her son, I don't know why I think it is a son, but I'm pretty sure. They are going to have a chicken dish that her son has made before. The recipe calls for jalapeños. He is looking for a jar of jalapeños. In the fridge. On the top shelf, maybe. Or in the door. He has found them. And dinner is saved.

#390

I tagged along to Dunkirk, I changed trains and I made it down to the harbor, but that was as far as I got. I had lost sight of the choirmaster long before we finally arrived there, but I found a hotel down by the harbor. It had a view of the sea, which was calm and gray. I had lost my desire for both annual meetings and boats by then. It had dawned on me that I had been lucky in Lille. That I could have woken up in a hotel room that was already occupied, where someone had gone to bed on the night of the seventeenth and where that same someone woke up in my bed on the morning of the eighteenth. In principle. If the day had conducted itself as one would expect. Fortunately, I had checked in early and must have been given a room where no one had been staying on the seventeenth of November.

It was late in the afternoon when I arrived at the Dunkirk hotel and this time I asked for a room where no one had stayed recently and which had not, therefore, been cleaned for a day or two. I said that I was allergic to certain cleaning products. I would be happy to pay extra.

The receptionist checked and gave me the all clear. There had been no one in the room I was given for the past three days. Luckily it was low season, he said. I located my room, let myself in and sat by the window with its view of the harbor until I began to feel cold because there was no heating in the room. I got into bed, slid under a duvet and a blue-checked bedspread and soon fell asleep.

This morning I woke alone to a pale gray morning and now I am moving on because I have found a train, a local train and we are traveling inland again. We stop at small stations, people get on and off, the seats are covered in a checked fabric and I sit here with my bag on the seat next to me, because there are not many passengers.

Today it is not a telephone conversation, but it might as well have been, because one person is doing the talking while the other is silent. The silent one is going to see a newly born grand-child, that much she has managed to say, but now she is merely listening. She is not the one with a story to tell. That is the man with the dogs. The woman listens politely, nodding occasion-ally. They are sitting opposite one another with a table between them as well as two large dogs, one grayish in color, the other speckled, lying on the floor under the table. The speckled dog is always sad, depressed almost, its owner says. Up until a few months ago he had had another dog and when it died the speck-led one had been heartbroken. A few weeks later he had brought home the gray dog. It was intended to be the speckled dog's new friend, but they are not friends yet.

I think they have noticed that I am listening to their conversa-tion, but what they cannot see is that I am writing down their conversation. I have a table in front of me and we can only see each other if I lean forward slightly and look across at them. The woman who is going to see her grandchild can sense that I am listening. She leans forward and shoots a glance at me, as if wishing to protect her fellow passenger, shield him from inquisitive ears, but I flick through my papers and look at my phone and she is given to understand that I am otherwise oc-cupied. Why would I be listening to them? A young woman with a black folder, papers and a large shoulder bag lying next to her, and a cell phone. The phone is no longer connected to the out-side world, but they can't see that.

The man had always thought he was his dogs' best friend. At night when he went to bed the dogs would lie down on either side of him: his old dog on the one side and the speckled one close beside him on the other. He felt loved. I lean forward a little and turn slightly. I can see his listener nodding. She can well understand that.

But when the older of the two dogs died the speckled one no longer wanted to sleep beside him on the bed. It was grieving, he said. It was inconsolable. He tried to get one dog to come up onto the bed, wanting to comfort it, he thought it liked him, that he was its best friend.

He wasn't. The dog had lain on his bed because it was the closest it could get to the other dog. I was just in the way, the dog owner said. It tolerated me, he said. But the speckled dog would really rather have been alone on the bed with the other dog. The one that had died. I was just in the way, he said, and when the old dog died the speckled one no longer had any reason to lie on the bed. It retreated to a blanket in the living room.

When he realized that his dogs had not loved him at all he got the gray dog, a sheepdog, he said, bending down and stroking the gray dog's long, wavy coat. That way at least the speckled dog would have a friend. Now they slept in their baskets in the living room. He slept alone in his bed.

His listener nodded but said nothing because the man with the dogs was not looking for sympathy, he was simply telling his story. The only thing that bothered him, he said, was that he had believed his dogs loved him so much that they wouldn't leave his side all night. He had been fooled. Which is to say his ego had fooled him, because his dogs had never said they loved him. The old dog had simply lain there, probably for warmth, or possibly out of habit and the speckled dog had never said it was lying there on his account.

I was not the only one who was listening. When the man was finished other passengers also looked away quickly and a woman a couple of seats away breathed a heavy sigh and gazed at the countryside. As for me, when his story came to an end I busied myself with my papers. I don't think the dog owner's listener knew what to say, either that or the conversation was simply over, and now they are looking out of the window while the man with the dogs pats the speckled one, which has got to its feet under the table.

#395

I am no longer carried along by streams of people. I don't need crowds to throw myself into. I don't need packed modes of transport. I am starting to like the midmorning traffic with its scattering of travelers, standard railroad carriages, slow-moving passengers with coffee cups and brown paper bags.

I listen. I sit with a book or my papers, and sometimes I jot something down, not always, but in the railroad carriage, with passengers dotted here and there, at small tables or pressed up against a window, there is an air of intimacy between us, we greet one another, a little nod, we are acquaintances for a moment, but then we withdraw. We have phones or books or papers to read. We have newspapers or headphones and laptops.

There is a woman whose house has been broken into and now she is on the phone, telling her story. She must have told it several times by now because there is nothing muddled about it. She has honed and polished her account, it doesn't jump about, it is neither faltering nor disjointed, she is no longer indignant or shocked.

She expects us to be listening, but she is not sure that we are. She glances around, there aren't many of us, possibly four or five within earshot. We are crossing borders, she is speaking French, but we will soon be in Germany, she has no way of knowing which of us speaks her language, but this is a story we are welcome to hear.

The listener on the phone has not heard it before, because there is an introduction and not a single detail is omitted. Details regarding the break-in: glass in the hallway, from the pane of glass in the door being smashed, and in her daughter's room, Sandrine's room, she says, Sandrine must be her daughter and her room had been turned upside down. Sandrine's little tins, they had searched everywhere. But not in the cookie tin, and all the money for her vacation had been in the cookie tin, so they hadn't found that. There was a faint note of triumph in her voice which makes me think that it was an expensive vacation and that there must have been quite a lot of money in the cookie tin. Then there is a pause. The story is clearly over. That detail about the cookie tin was the finale, it hangs in the air for a moment, an odd conclusion, it doesn't seem like the end of a conversation, more like a fanfare, a triumph. There is silence, but her listener is evidently not saying anything because the burgled woman doesn't reply, it is just a pause.

Then she changes the subject because there are arrangements to be made: a girls' night out, an old friends' get-together. It occurs to me that there was no explanation for the cookie tin. Where was it and why did the thieves not find it? The listener must have been familiar with the tin because no explanation for it was forthcoming and the burgled woman segued almost seamlessly from Sandrine's collection of tins to the cookie tin. From the child's room to the kitchen probably, because if there had been a cookie tin somewhere else, in the living room or the hallway, for example, it would surely have stuck out like a sore thumb. But who collects cash for a vacation in a cookie tin, and who keeps enough cash in a cookie tin to pay for a vacation?

Granted, I have a bag full of cash myself. Each day I withdraw as much as I can, because you never know when you may need money. Do I know whether my credit cards will last forever? But that is different, I feel. I would never hide cash in a cookie tin. Maybe the thieves wouldn't either. Maybe that's why they didn't find it. Maybe I am more like the thieves, stealing people's lives? They have set out their cookie tins in the railroad carriage, but that doesn't necessarily mean you can help yourself. Maybe they would be delighted to serve the whole railroad carriage, I don't know. I don't know whether I am stealing or simply accepting what is being passed around.

But then the conversation came to an end, the burgled woman was getting off the train. I looked out of the window. We were in Aachen, but I stayed where I was, I could think of no reason to get off, so I let the burgled woman go.

#398

Today there is a young woman whose boyfriend has forsaken her. She can't be very old. Twenty-five maybe. Twenty-two. Maybe younger. Younger than me, anyway. She is younger and more forsaken. Not that I noticed this at first, when I opened the door of the train car. It was a regional train and she was sitting by herself in a six-person compartment with two large suitcases on the floor beside her.

There were no standard railroad carriages on this train so I had sidled along a narrow, suitcase-strewn corridor, past almost full compartments. The curtain in her compartment was drawn halfway across the window, I might have guessed that this meant she wanted to be alone, but I am not used to these trains, they feel like a relic of a bygone age when people could hide behind curtains in small railway compartments. I felt as if I were intruding, as if I were taking one of her seats, but I opened the door and went in anyway.

When I opened the door and asked if the other seats were free she nodded forlornly and I could tell that something was wrong. At first I thought she simply wanted to have the compartment to herself and I nearly left again, but there had already been four or five people in the compartment next door, so I edged my way in with my bag and sat down on the seat nearest the door with the bag on my lap.

It took me a little while to grasp what was wrong, but I sensed right away that it was fragility, not possessiveness that led her to guard the compartment. It made me feel like an intruder but here I am, and it would be rude to leave now, so I sit and make notes on a book I am reading. I have a dictionary with me and I have taken that and my book out of my bag. I read a bit, then put the book down and write a few lines, check my dictionary then read a bit more, or appear to do so.

I bought the books in Bonn. I had followed a couple of very talkative passengers, the one French, the other German, or maybe they were both. They switched from the one language to the other several times in the course of their conversation and when we reached the station I went into the nearest bookshop. I picked up a dictionary and when I went to pay there was a pile of Goethe's *Elective Affinities* next to the cash register. It was the sound of the German title I liked: *Die Wahlverwandtschaften*. To begin with, this book may merely have been an excuse for taking notes and looking up German words in my dictionary, but I have now started reading it. I read slowly, I read on trains and in hotel rooms. I travel from place to place and yesterday I arrived in Hanover. I spent the night in a hotel near the station and bought a ticket on a northbound train, a morning train, but it was canceled and we were directed to another platform, so suddenly there were more passengers than expected at eleven a.m. on a normal day.

It did not take long for me to learn my forlorn fellow passenger's story, not because she told it to me, but it was easy to grasp the gist and not hard to understand even with my limited German.

The forsaken young woman is on her way home to her parents' and she has already spoken to her mother twice. Her boyfriend has just left her, she had not seen it coming at all, in fact they had been getting on really well. I can tell that this catastrophe is very fresh, possibly from this morning, or yesterday evening, and she needs to relate all the details to her mother and to me. She is going to Bremen. It will be another two hours before she is there, that is a long time to travel with a broken heart.

I think of catastrophes great and small. I think of my own. I think of fresh catastrophes and of those that have had time to take shape. The catastrophe in the railway compartment is slight and breathless, it possesses details that would be private were they not so fresh. Perhaps she thinks I cannot understand her because I spoke to her in English when I entered the compartment. But it makes no difference. I am not here. I don't think it matters whether I am here or not. In her world there is only a stunned daughter and a listening mother.

They had thought of having children. Not right away, but they had talked about it. There had been a future. She had already bought his Christmas present. There had been *Kinder* and *Weihnachtsgeschenke* in their life. November is possibly a little early for Christmas presents, I think to myself. But there had been plans. There had been a shared apartment and she couldn't understand why he had left. That was the worst part, that she didn't understand why. She had been standing on the steps when he told her. Which steps? The ones outside the station? Perhaps the breakup was as fresh as that, perhaps he had walked her to the station and then told her that he was leaving her. Where was she going when he told her? Home to see her parents? Had he walked her to the station and then told her that he no longer wanted to be with her? On the steps outside the station? On the steps leading to the platform? And why such large suitcases? Maybe he told her yesterday evening. During the night she packed the essentials. Or possibly everything. And now she is going home.

A refreshments cart came through the train while the forlorn young woman was telling her mother that she wouldn't need to buy her neighbor's high chair. What neighbor asks such a question: my grandchildren are all grown now and you don't have any yet, but won't you buy my high chair? As if children are going to come along if you buy your neighbor's high chair. And why had her mother told her about the neighbor's high chair? The neighbors have a high chair for sale, should I buy it? Or had the mother said something about it when her daughter told her about the breakup? So I won't need to buy my neighbor's high chair after all?

When the compartment door slid open I ordered a cup of tea and asked my fellow passenger if I could get her a cup too. She declined, but politely. She smiled a little wanly, as if to say that it was all right for me to be there. As if that was what I had asked: may I be here?

I don't know, but now I am sitting here with a cup of tea and juggling my papers. I put the paper cup on the floor in front of me and bend down to pick it up when I want to sip my tea. I have the urge to do something for her. Although I know there is nothing I can do. Nor do I need to. Maybe it would be better if I left.

Instead I have spread myself out a bit in the compartment. I have placed my coat on the seat opposite me and my bag on the floor. We are taking up most of the compartment now. I guard her space so she won't have to cope with any more travelers.

People walk back and forth along the corridor. If I leave the compartment someone else will move in. That would be worse, I tell myself. She has just got used to me. Or maybe it would make no difference. Now I am sitting leaning against the curtain. It is striped in pale brown and beige. I think of *Weihnachtsgeschenke* and drink my tea out of a paper cup, and every now and again I write a few sentences on a piece of paper that I have folded and slipped into my book.

#399

At Bremen we left the train. I held back in the narrow corridor outside the compartments and let the forsaken young woman get out first. I kept my distance. I was merely a listener, not family, but I wanted to make sure that she was in good hands before I let her go.

Her mother was on the platform, a woman in beige, in a trouser suit with tan shoes and a red scarf around her neck. She did not look like a woman who would take time off to see to her jilted daughter, or who dreamt of having grandchildren, but now she was hugging the girl and shortly afterward I saw them wheeling two large suitcases through the station, out of the door and over to the parking lot, where they found one of the biggest cars there, which was lucky, because they would need plenty of room for those suitcases.

Once I had seen them get into the car and turn away from the station I walked up into the city center and soon found a hotel where I was given a room overlooking the street. I checked that no one had stayed there for the past couple of days, took the stairs up to my room and let myself in.

From the room I could look down onto the street and the traffic, both trams and cars, passing up and down, and I could see a square where workers were busy hanging lights in the trees. A little early for that, I thought, as I boiled water in a kettle and observed their neatly coordinated work, but they probably needed to start now if the whole city was to be illuminated in December.

I was tired but I had had nothing since breakfast except two cups of tea. So I went out to get something to eat and as soon as I returned to my room I climbed into bed. I thought of *Weihnachtsgeschenke* and *Wahlverwandtschaften* and fell fast asleep.

Now I am sitting by the window, gazing out at the empty square across the road from the hotel and the trams running back and forth. Lined up on the sidewalk across the road are lots of garbage bags in different colors. Waiting to be picked up by a garbage truck. I sit here waiting for electricians and cranes and hydraulic platforms that haven't yet arrived. I think of December. I think of *heute* and *morgen* and *übermorgen*. I think of *gestern* and *vorgestern*. And now I am also thinking of *Frühstück*.

#401

Today I have a goal. I am going somewhere. Home, I could say. But I no longer know what home means. Home was Clairon-sous-Bois, but not anymore, and now I am on my way to Brussels. That too was home. Once upon a time. Home is no longer a place to go. But today I have a direction. With me I have presents. They are in two large shopping bags in the luggage rack.

#402

Anyone would think it was Christmas, my mother said when she saw the presents in the shopping bags. They were all carefully wrapped, most of them in Christmas paper. It felt a little too warm for Christmas. I spotted leaves on some of the trees in the garden, and on the rambling rose over by the shed a single rose was in bloom, defying the autumn cold. On the way up to the house I noticed that a few yellow fruits still clung to the bare branches of the quince bush beside the garden path, although most of them had fallen off and lay gleaming on the ground under the bush. There was a bit of a breeze. It was not what you could call winter and it would be up to me to provide some Christmas spirit.

My mother was in the garden when I arrived. She had taken most of the day off because the pupils at the international school where she teaches had been on a trip. She had only been at work for a couple of hours and when she got back she had gone straight out into the garden. Now she came walking toward me carrying a bowl for the yellow quinces. It was hard to hug with all the shopping bags between us, plus the bowl and my mother's gestures of surprise. The presents were for later, I told her once we were in the house and had put everything down in the kitchen.

We must have Lisa over, I said. My sister. We should give her a call. My mother had spoken to her only the day before. We should ask her to come for dinner. This evening, or tomorrow if I stay that long. Probably tomorrow, I said. I meant the eighteenth, but I also meant Christmas Eve. My mother meant the nineteenth of November.

We had supper when my father got home from work an hour later. We ate at the table in the living room. My mother never got around to gathering her quinces because we ended up having coffee instead.

While we ate I told my parents that I had some business to take care of in Brussels. Some books to pick up. We talked about ordinary things: my father's day at work and my mother's day off, my sister's studies and T. & T. Selter. We didn't talk about a time that had ground to a halt, but we did talk about my fellow travelers. I had been traveling quite a lot recently, I said, and then I told them about the mournful dog, about break-ins and cookie tins and sailing-club board meetings. I mimed my fellow passengers' conversations, putting my hand to my ear like a cell phone and patting an invisible dog under a table. I told them about the forlorn girl in the railway compartment, about *Weihnachtsgeschenke* and *Wahlverwandtschaften*: how I liked the sound of the words, and maybe the rhythm, and that I had read Goethe and given the appearance of making notes on what I was reading because I wasn't sure whether my fellow passengers were actually telling their stories to me. In a way I felt that I was stealing from them. I didn't want to be caught with my fingers in the cookie tin, so to speak.

My father did not think it was stealing. He felt, rather, that the broadcasting of private phone conversations in public spaces was theft. Of other people's peace and quiet, their privacy, possibly even their humanity. As if the speaker was sitting in their own private space and regarded the other passengers as fixtures and fittings: like a door, a seat, a luggage rack, he said. As if fellow passengers were not people but objects. My mother chimed in, citing the example of children at her school who were often delivered to the school gates by parents with cell phones in their hands. As if the children were packages being dispatched or bags of shopping being carried home. I thought of my woebegone fellow passenger and her broken heart. Had I been a shopping bag in the corner? A luggage rack? Or more like a curtain that could be drawn across the compartment window? I don't know, but my parents had already changed the subject.

I don't know if they are right, and I don't know if I have anything against being a curtain, but it was suddenly late in the evening and I went off to bed in my old room. It hasn't changed much since I left home. My bed and my desk are still there and, apart from bookshelves along one wall containing the house's overspill of books, everything is almost the same as when I was still living at home.

I was up early this morning. Just after six by the kitchen clock. I made coffee and sat down at the table in the corner. I hesitated for a second before taking the place that has always been my mother's, but the table had been pushed up against the wall and the place where I used to sit as a child had been squashed flat. I was struck by how strange it felt to sit there on my mother's chair, wrong really, because for as long as I can remember we had all had our set places at the table: my father and I against the wall, my mother across from my father and my sister next to her. Here we had sat every morning and every evening over a mixture—a *pêle-mêle* as my mother would say—of English and Belgian meals and in a mixture of English and French words. My parents had met when my father was on holiday in England. My mother lived in Suffolk, but she moved to Brussels to be with my father as soon as she finished college and my sister and I had always lived with these mixtures at the kitchen table. But our places were fixed, a solid family square, and I have no memory of any other tables or places because we moved to this house when I was little and this is the same table as we had back then.

After my sister and I moved out, the table was pushed up against the wall, giving more space in the kitchen. And for a few years it was pushed back and forth, when we were home on visits. There were times when we both came home to stay for a few months, often in the summer, and then all four of us would sit around the table again.

Now, though, I think the table is pushed up against the wall most of the time. I think my parents sit at right angles to one another when they eat, but I am not sure, and when we come to visit we usually eat at the dining table in the living room.

At around seven o'clock my mother came into the kitchen. Surprised, but not surprised enough for me to feel that I had to explain my presence. Well, you know where the spare key is. And the bed linens. And the coffee. She said this with a happy note in her voice, which made me feel welcome, as if she regarded my intrusion as a sign that the family was still intact and that the place I had usurped would always be mine on special occasions.

She discreetly asked after Thomas, as if to check that nothing was wrong and I assured her that he was waiting for me in Clairon. She looked relieved and I thought of the young woman on the train and her mother who would, for a while, have to wave goodbye to her dreams of grandchildren and high chairs, because even though my mother never says anything I think she does wonder, now and again, whether that high chair in the attic will ever be used again.

A moment later my father appeared, equally surprised, but instantly assuming that my arrival had been engineered by my mother so that we could spend her day off together. He hoped, though, he said, that I would stay for a few days, or till the following day at least, because he had to go, he had a ten o'clock meeting, but he would be back as soon as he could.

So I told them anyway. Over breakfast. That it was Christmas. That I had brought presents. That time had fallen apart. That I had been counting the days and, if I had counted correctly, today should be Christmas Eve. That I had spent day after day with Thomas. That I had moved to the rue de l'Ermitage and been to Paris and been carried along by random travelers. That time passed and passed and yet didn't pass at all.

I reassured them. No one was dead, no one was hurt. It was merely a fault in time. I said that I had got used to that thought. That I was a different person. That a path had been cleared in my head, snow shoveled, scrub cleared. That I was trying to find a way, that I wanted to return to a normal timescale, but that I needed Christmas, needed time to pass, needed not to be stuck in one endless November day. I said that they could help me with December.

After breakfast my father left for his meeting, promising to be back as soon as he could. My mother and I made up a list of things for dinner and my mother went off to do the shopping. She had a bit of paperwork and some assignments to drop off at the school, but she wouldn't be long. I had borrowed her phone and while she was away I called my sister and told her the whole story. She was meant to be at the university, where she was studying chemistry, but now she would take the day off to spend Christmas with her family.

My mother got back, having picked up both a turkey and Brussels sprouts. She had also managed to rustle up a Christmas pudding and a Bûche de Noël even though it was still only November. Our Christmas had always been a mixture: always presents and turkey on Christmas Eve and leftovers for lunch on Christmas Day. With Christmas pudding. And a small gift for everyone on Christmas morning to keep up the British tradition. That and the Brussels sprouts that we dutifully ate with the turkey on Christmas Eve. With the Christmas pudding we had vanilla ice cream, not custard—or crème anglaise as my father called it—because my mother had never liked custard. And there were always roast potatoes, which we all loved, and lots of them so there would be enough for the next day as well. So our Christmas consisted of two traditions: Christmas and Noël, two Christmases and two stodgy desserts, with little harmony or balance. But traditions don't need to harmonize, they simply have to be there. They have to be there as a sort of safety net, to give one something to land on. When the world falls apart. When time fractures.

It feels as though something has been repaired, now, as I sit in my old room, thinking of Christmas and Noël. Of how things that don't really go together can, nonetheless, be combined. My mother and father. Me and my sister. The eighteenth of November and Christmas Eve, which we still managed to combine. Almost.

We made Christmas dinner as if everything was perfectly normal. I am deft at roast potatoes. I have been since I was ten and I am always responsible for that part of the dinner. As soon as he got back my father started on the Brussels sprouts. Lisa was in charge of the turkey. It was only midafternoon when she put it in the oven, and even though she had full control of the situation we all hovered around the beast, turning it or sticking a meat thermometer into it every now and again.

It was late before we eventually sat down to turkey with roast potatoes and Bûche de Noël. We ate at the table in the living room, because that too was part of the Christmas ritual. I insisted on giving them presents, lots of presents, because I had bags full of them.

I would rather not think about Thomas, but I do anyway. As something missing. He would have eaten my roast potatoes and said that I ought to make them more often, not only at Christmas. He would have eaten Lisa's roast bird with relish, he would have eaten his Brussels sprouts without comment, but he would have asked for the quince jelly which is a special tradition in our family, not one that goes far back in one branch of our family tree or another, but a tradition that came into being solely because there was a quince bush in the front garden when we moved into this house. Every autumn my mother has gathered the yellow quinces, at first because she felt she ought to, then out of habit, and now as a reminder of the years that have gone. In the spring the quince bush sports its red flowers, later the reddish-green leaves and the small green fruit and then the yellowish-green quinces, large and lone or in little clusters close-packed along the branches. In the autumn when they are ripe and yellow they drop to the ground under the bush and at some point, sometimes not until late November or even December, the golden quinces with their waxy and slightly greasy skins are gathered. First they sit in a bowl in the kitchen, emitting their distinctive scent, their skin turning brown in places, and finally, in a process that can take a couple of days, my mother will make them into a clear, dark-red jelly, the color of which is still a mystery to me: how can yellow fruit produce such a dark-red jelly? Over the years the bush has spread, it has sent up shoots and been cut back, and a couple of years ago, when we moved into the house in Clairon, Thomas asked if he could have a shoot for the garden there. He was given four, which he planted and declared that sooner or later one of us would learn the art of making quince jelly and carry on the tradition. But there was no quince jelly for Christmas dinner this year because the quinces were still lying out there in the dark, and in any case the tradition is only a tradition because there happened to be a quince bush in the garden.

We didn't talk much about the fault in time over dinner. I had explained most of it and I think my parents needed a while to absorb what had happened. Lisa was more interested in the basic principles, the actual mechanics of it, which we had discussed on several occasions during the day, and at one point, when she and I were in the kitchen, putting the leftovers from dinner in the fridge, she suggested that she could join me on my travels. I said I wasn't sure that would be possible, but if it was I would have to explain the whole thing to her again every morning. I told her that I had tried to persuade Thomas to go to Paris with me. But that he had demurred. He had no wish to be drawn into my November day. But Lisa did not demur. She thought it would be possible. She made it sound like a vacation. She talked about going south, about warmth and sunshine. She needed a vacation, she was in the midst of finishing her dissertation. Maybe she could carry on working on that, she said. There was still quite a bit of writing to be done. I could help her. I told her that whatever she wrote would only disappear during the night, but she thought there was a way around that problem. I could write everything down on paper and sleep with the papers under my pillow and the next day she would have got a little further without any time having passed. All while we soaked up the southern sun. But I am not going south. I long for December and January. I long for the year to start moving.

Just after midnight, when Lisa had gone home and my parents were asleep, I went into the kitchen. I took a cooler bag from a hook inside the broom closet and got the leftovers from Christmas dinner out of the fridge to put in the bag, because I had no faith in the ability of the fridge to retain them. In the freezer I found two large ziplock bags of chicken soup. I laid one of these in the bottom of the bag and the other up against the side of it. Lisa had put the leftover turkey in a plastic tub along with some cold Brussels sprouts. I placed this in the cooler bag and alongside it I put four large potatoes which I had managed to squeeze into another plastic tub. There was no room for more so I left the rest in the fridge. On top of all this I laid the last of our Bûche de Noël, still in its box.

All of a sudden, as I was zipping the cooler bag shut, I felt laughter bubbling up. My eye had fallen on the Christmas pudding in its box on the kitchen countertop, and I realized that if I wanted to have Christmas pudding on Christmas Day I would have to take it to bed with me. I put my hand over my mouth so as not to laugh out loud and risk waking anyone with the giggles that were now breaking free and rising up from deep down inside me. I felt them bubbling up from the pit of my stomach and into my chest. I gurgled my way through a brief bout of laughter with my hand over my mouth: it felt more like sobbing, a stifled, mirthful fit of weeping, compressed and carefree, gurgling Christmas sobs that mocked all of my efforts to hold time together. I laughed at my earnestness and my insistence on keeping the Christmas customs and again I was conscious of my feelings—the whole gamut: mirth, despair, a welter of sadness and happiness and sudden laughter, all entering the scene on my Christmas night.

It went on for a few minutes and left me with a feeling of lightness, and just as my laughter subsided the fridge started up with a sound that seemed at first like the usual mechanical hum of a refrigerator but then changed pitch, suddenly sounding exactly like my laughter, half giggling, half sobbing. Possibly a little more mechanical than mine, possibly a little louder, and the fridge made no attempt to stifle its giggles. It just stood there, upright, emitting its stuttering, almost sobbing laugh. As if it had been smitten. As if it was laughing along with me. Or crying. But that's all right. It is quite permissible for a fridge that cannot hold on to its Christmas food to laugh—or cry—like a human being if it so wishes.

I am sitting in my old room. I have placed our Christmas pudding at the foot of the bed under my duvet and the cooler bag containing the leftovers from the evening's dinner is under my bed. With any luck Christmas can continue tomorrow, Christmas Day, because there are leftovers, and Christmas pudding, and now I have done what I can to keep Christmas going. I have my duvet drawn up around me, I have a pillow at my back and a sheaf of paper resting on Volume I of the *Encyclopaedia Britannica*, which my parents have consigned to my old room, and it feels as if nothing can get at me here. It feels both carefree and very solemn. Christmas Night, tucked in between a pillow and an encyclopedia, with paper that remembers everything people forget and a Christmas pudding in a box at the foot of my bed.

I left the presents in the living room, even though they are bound to disappear. There is no point in giving presents that you have already given once so I crumpled up the wrapping paper and threw it into the trash can out by the garden shed. The remains of our Christmas dinner are the main thing because having the leftovers the next day is all part of Christmas. Maybe that is what we celebrate. That there is always something left over. That we carry something away with us. Maybe that is why the fridge joined in with its sobbing laughter.

The fridge is silent now. I tiptoed past it and across to my parents' bedroom. I stood for a moment looking at them in their bed: my parents, fast asleep, each making their own sound, two different sounds which I had never noticed as a child, possibly because it was always me sleeping and them listening, or maybe these are sounds they have acquired with age.

I got myself a glass of water from the kitchen and drew the curtains in my room. They are the same curtains as when I was a teenager, the same wallpaper too: a diagonal pattern in a kind of dusty pink, bordering on beige. I remember it as being a deeper shade of pink, but I am probably mistaken.

#403

Our Christmas morning began a little chaotically. My parents had forgotten everything. I had to tell them the whole story again, from my burned hand to the mirthful fridge, before we could even have breakfast.

They got up while I was making a pot of far too strong coffee and yet again they were not as surprised as I had expected. My mother was clearly happy that I could still turn up unannounced and my father thought my mother had known I was coming. To start with, we sat around the kitchen table, drinking strong coffee while I repeated the long explanation which they had already been given the day before, but which now also included our day on Christmas Eve, that evening and my encounter with the fridge. Toward the end of my account my mother began to grow impatient. She got out bread and apricot jam while my father called to cancel the meeting he was due to attend and when he returned to the kitchen he made more coffee, not quite as strong as mine, and we ate bread and jam while they both tried to take in my story, asking questions about certain details, some more relevant than others, and making various suggestions, all of which I naturally had to say that I had already considered or tried.

After the coffee and apricot jam we went straight on to the Christmas Eve leftovers, which my father poked at a bit even though I assured him that it had all remained refrigerated overnight, albeit in a cooler bag, so it was perfectly safe to eat. The leftovers had stayed cold in my room, the bags of chicken soup which I had used as cooling elements were only partially defrosted and I had put them back in the freezer. Although I don't think it was the health risk he was worried about. His reluctance probably had more to do with his not being used to eating leftovers from a meal he had partaken of, but of which he had no memory.

I had heated up the potatoes in the oven, but my mother didn't think four potatoes was enough. She retrieved another three, which I had left in the fridge because they wouldn't fit into my plastic tub and which, to my surprise, had not disappeared, although, as I told them when explaining the workings of the eighteenth of November, that was probably because I had been the one to cook them. So then I had to explain this peculiar phenomenon, that the transition from the one time to the other was not clear-cut, that it was not purely mechanical, that it was—or at least this was how I explained it to my father—more of an optical thing, a sort of dissolve or parallel shift, a sort of interweaving of the two times, where my progressive time, my interaction with the world, my consuming and accumulating time, while it certainly contrasted with the forgetfulness of the rest of the world, does not follow a set of automatic or inviolable rules and laws, adhering instead to certain rough principles, rules girded by a zone of indecisiveness, an uncertainty which I could not quite fathom but which typically, as with those roast potatoes, formed a demarcation line between those parts of the world that I had had a hand in, so to speak, and those that simply returned to their starting point.

I explained to my father that it was there, at the interface between the two times, that the uncertainty lay, but this explanation did not satisfy him. I insisted that there were no fixed rules. It was not mechanical. The Brussels sprouts that he had prepared and cooked the day before, even though he could not remember doing so, and the remains of the turkey that had sat in the oven, with all of us taking turns to check on it and turn it and prick it with a fork, might well have stayed put in the fridge. But I had not wanted to take the chance, I said. If I had not kept the turkey and the cold Brussels sprouts in the cooler bag in my room and put the Christmas pudding at the foot of my bed he might have had nothing but some rather dry potatoes to poke at now. Everything else would have vanished and we would have no leftovers to eat. Although I was not sure of this. I had a feeling that the things I undertook with Thomas were more stable than, for example, my shifting of the gas heater with Marie in the shop on my first eighteenth of November, and that might also be the case with a Christmas Eve dinner that you made with your family. But I had had no interest in experimenting with the festive leftovers and running the risk of them disappearing.

My father still felt that he was eating the remains of someone else's dinner, which didn't really bother him, he said, as long as he didn't have to imagine that it was his own Christmas dinner he had in front of him on the eighteenth of November.

My mother thought the situation regarding objects sounded more like a teaching exercise, as if the objects were subject to a form of communication, a learning process, whereby the things of the world had to be trained, or possibly even persuaded to stay and that there was no one specific way of doing this, but that some adaptation of the different objects was necessary. She had no problem with the idea of the transition from the one time to the other not being automatic. Of there being an element of uncertainty. Neither did my father, or so he maintained, and then they fell to discussing the difference between the two ways of viewing objects, all in an atmosphere of amicable disagreement, as if the gray zone inhabited by the objects were just another of the small questions of everyday life: on a par with the question as to the right amount of coffee beans for a beaker of French press coffee or how best to get your teenage daughters to help with the household chores. Measurement or intuition, training or rules and, as so often before, I heard how they each changed their stance, because, if one of them went too far in one direction, the other would imperceptibly adopt the abandoned viewpoint, so that the balance was upheld.

Our conversation did not get much further than this balance, because it was time to put on our Christmas pudding, which was still lying at the foot of my bed and would have to sit and steam for at least two hours.

This time we decided not to call Lisa. I had told my parents that she had been thinking of coming with me when I left. This did not go over well. I told them that it wasn't catching, that I was hardly likely to drag her into my recurring day, but they felt that we should keep Lisa out of it.

I did not mention the presents because they were gone, of course, and no one could remember what they had been given. Besides, I now had other, better ideas for gifts. But those would have to wait till next Christmas, I told myself.

Instead, while my father minded the Christmas pudding, which was simmering away on the stove, my mother and I went into town. She wanted to give me a present, she said. She wanted to buy me a dress. Or something else, if I would rather have something else. I think she would have given me anything to keep me from taking her younger daughter away with me into the unknown, and I didn't have the heart to tell her that I could buy all the dresses I wanted. Whether they would stay with me was another matter. That would require a certain amount of persuasion, some insight into how things behave, into the training of inanimate objects.

I found a grayish blue, wool-mix dress which I could wear along with the black dress I had worn every day since I left Paris and which I had occasionally rinsed out in a sink with soap or shampoo from the hotels I had stayed at. I don't know whether I can hold on to a new dress if I don't wear it all the time, but I have put the new one on closest to my skin and am counting on it staying with me. A grayish-blue border sticks out below the hem of my old dress, but it looks as though it is meant to be that way. No one can tell that I am training a dress to stay with me.

In the same shop I also found some woolen underwear: a long-sleeved top and leggings that I can wear under my other clothes when winter comes. Winter has been on my mind ever since I had the urge to celebrate Christmas and when I saw the underwear I knew that I would have to get myself seasons. I needed warm clothes and weather to go with them. True, we had celebrated a Christmas of sorts, and still to come was the concluding Christmas pudding, now keeping warm on the stove, but the weather in Brussels was too autumnal, there were too many leaves on the trees and quinces on the ground.

My mother said she hoped I would find my way back to normal time. That she believed I would. I had always gone my own way, she said. I am not sure what she meant by that, nor do I know if she is right, but I made no comment. Just then we were interrupted by a shop assistant and soon afterward we were walking along the street and getting on a bus that took us out to the suburbs.

It was late in the afternoon when we got back. The sky was growing dark and the quinces glowed yellow under the almost bare bush when we walked up the garden path. We had our Christmas pudding and later in the evening we picked the last bits of meat off the turkey carcass and made up some sandwiches. We weren't particularly hungry, not after the heavy pudding, which we had had without the vanilla ice cream that my mother had bought, because it had of course disappeared from the freezer during the night, I had forgotten about that, but it was too late, no one felt like running out to get ice cream. We were all tired, I think, and by ten o'clock we were saying good night and getting ready for bed.

My mother came into my room after I had gone to bed and sat down in the chair next to me, as she had often done when I was a child—and right up until I left home, in fact—and I felt the confusion of the half-grown child: torn between the wish that she would go away and let me get on with a life in which she no longer had any part and the powerful urge to sink into a world in which all the big problems are taken care of by the grown-ups. And probably, in this case, the hope that she, my mother, could set time to rights and then slip back out of the room. Like the incident, on a school trip, when one of her young pupils dislocated his arm. Lisa and I had also been on the trip and we stood and watched while my mother put the limb back into place. I was amazed and proud when I saw the relief on the face of the shocked boy, whose arm had been sitting at such an odd angle. She had used a particular move, both sharp and gentle, more of a lift than a tug and suddenly the arm was back in place. That's what mothers do, I must have thought at the time. It made me strangely at peace with the world to know that my mother could put dislocated limbs back into place.

But there was not much she could do about the repetitions of time. We talked a little about the possibility of us being back to normal time as early as tomorrow, out of the loop, the coil, the repetition, or whatever you call it, but it was more of an obligatory conversation in which we each had our lines, the sort of game of make-believe one might play with one's parents. I remember how we used to play at restaurants: my father with a folded tea towel over his arm and Lisa and I writing menus offering outlandish dishes at crazy prices. We had just been playing at Christmas: first Christmas Eve, then Christmas Day and now we were playing that there was a way out. My parents had joined in the game and my mother had played along right up to the thought that it would soon be over, that we would wake up to the nineteenth of November or maybe even to the twenty-sixth of December, Boxing Day as she called it. But more than anything I think she was simply relieved that we had got through the day without me involving my sister and possibly even taking her away with me. I said I hoped she would get her quinces gathered and make her jelly—then I would come back for Christmas.

I would find a way out, I said. I was sure there would be an answer. Out there somewhere there would be a solution. And I would find it. I would keep traveling, I would keep my eyes open, I would listen to people's conversations. With a dictionary. There would be something I could use. The world is full of good advice if you listen, I said.

I don't know why I said that. I was starting to think about where I should go. I was thinking about the trains and the passengers and clutched at the first thing that came to mind, hoping to re-assure her.

She hadn't thought of that, she said. That the problems in life might perhaps be solved by listening. Through conversations with family and friends, perhaps, yes. But she wasn't sure what one could learn from chance conversations between other people.

I said I was sure that through careful listening you could solve any problem that might arise. If you really listened. The great questions in life. Everything. And if you couldn't find it in people's conversations you could try listening to birdsong. Or the sound of the wind. You will always find your way to something.

I was well aware that I was taking the conversation down a sidetrack because I had not been thinking of traveling around listening to my fellow passengers at all. Or to the wind, for that matter. I felt like an adolescent who has come out with some comment and then has to back it up, partly out of defiance and partly to avoid having to make my mother privy to the thought that was now starting to overwhelm me: the thought that no matter what I did, whether I listened or not, I was never going to escape from the eighteenth of November.

I said I knew she felt differently. That in her view there was only one way to solve the world's problems, because she has always believed that all change has to start in a small way. With the children. That nothing will change until we realize this and abandon our misguided approach to the world's newest individuals.

My mother seemed relieved when I turned the conversation to the subject around which her whole life had revolved for as long as I could remember. The children. Her pupils, her own children, all the children in the world. In her life, every day was Christmas, I asserted, because every time a child was born she saw this as yet another opportunity to make the world a better place. In fact, she believed—and this she freely admitted— that if we seized this opportunity again and again, every time it came along, we would see changes, very gradually, one step at a time. War, violence, abuse of power, corruption, all would be reduced, making it easier to solve other problems: hunger, disease and poverty, all manner of ills. She has always believed this. I think it goes back to her own childhood and school days and I think she seriously believes it: that children who are not damaged along the way will automatically make the world a better place.

I asked her if that was how she saw the world, if it really was that simple, and she said she really believed it was. Simple, that is, she said, not easy. But, she insisted, that did not mean allowing a state of nature to prevail. Not at all. Children had to be helped and guided.

I stopped her there because I already knew her views on the necessary ingredients for the raising and schooling of children. Things like children having to learn several languages and how to tend a garden, like singing and music and the idea that children had to be helped to get through their formative years unbroken and intact, but not untested or unseasoned. With care, like plants, she always said, but before she could get started I told her that I regarded her way of thinking as a kind of mechanism, a gentle mechanism to be sure, a kind of redeemer mechanism whereby the children would save the world. A simple Christmas mechanism, I said, even though I knew she didn't like her way of thinking being described as mechanical. That was what my father and my sister believed: that technology would help us.

Then I asked her. Did she dream of grandchildren? Did she dream of getting the high chair down from the attic? She didn't know. More than anything she wanted her own children to be happy. And to help her pupils on their way. Possibly repair some damage here and there. One day, she said, she would like to have grandchildren, of course, but right now she was content with the children she had.

While she was talking I had slid down under my quilt and now she tucked it in around me as if I was just a little child. Then, suddenly, she began to sing *In the Bleak Midwinter*, very softly, almost like a lullaby.

In the bleak midwinter
Frosty wind made moan;
Earth stood hard as iron,
Water like a stone;
Snow had fallen, snow on snow,
Snow on snow,
In the bleak midwinter,
Long ago.

She sang the whole thing from start to finish, all five verses, and I could not help but sing along. We have always sung this carol at Christmastime so I sat up in bed and joined in. I took the alto part, as I have done ever since my mother gave up trying to get my voice to reach the heights of the melody and instead taught me to maintain the balance in the middle. My mother and Lisa always sang the melody, my father would growl some bass notes in the background, so my job was to keep the whole thing together in the middle and neither fall in with the melody nor my father's growling bass. Now we sang it without the bass part and by the time we reached the end we had almost got the harmonies right.

When we reached the end she said good night and left the room and not long afterward I got up and put on the new dress. I slipped my old dress over it and packed the woolen underwear into my bag.

I waited until the house was quiet and I figured that they would both be fast asleep then I crept into their room to listen to their sounds. Both sleep sounds were there, an uneven choir made up of two parents who have been playing at Christmas with their two grown-up children.

In the broom closet I found a flashlight, which I took with me. I gathered up my things and borrowed a couple of books from the bookshelves in my room. I had suddenly remembered that I had said I was going to pick up some books in Brussels. Now that is true. I have picked up books from their bookshelves and I am sitting on the bed, waiting. I have removed all traces of my visit, I have packed the last of our Christmas pudding into a plastic tub and put it in my bag. I am waiting for the night to erase all memory of our eighteenth of November and before anyone is awake I will leave the house.

#404

Now, sitting on the train, I think of my family as a solid core with friable edges. Something seems always to be crumbling away.

I think of wallpaper that is fading. I think of my mother's cigarette, which would often sit smoking away while she was busy with something else. The ash, which reached like a long gray finger into the ashtray until it was blown over and disintegrated.

I think of the two cubes of sugar that my father still dissolves in his coffee, the faint tinkle of the teaspoon and the sugar cubes in the cup, the sound of the sugar growing fainter and fainter until at last it is gone and only the sound of the teaspoon remains.

I think of hot baths and Lisa and me in the bathtub. We had these bath paints that could be used on the tiles around the tub and which would end up running together and turning into a brown soup, and when we were done we would pull the plug and let the soup drain away. On other occasions we took a comic or a toy-shop catalog into the bath with us and when we were finished reading we dissolved them in the water: we laid a page or two on top of the water, the paper would go soft, then the colors would run and gradually it would all melt into gray flakes and little clumps of soggy paper.

I think of the languages in our house, the linguistic confusion, a swirl of words and phrases that could be combined and swapped around, a language with fluid edges and free movement as long we stayed within the four walls of our house. When we went outside, though, there were compartments. At our school we spoke French and when we visited England everything was in English. In the land of the monoglots, as my mother would say, where we quickly learned to follow the proper linguistic etiquette, because no one understood us until we said *please* and *thank you*.

And now I am thinking of the compost bin in the garden, into which branches and leaves, dead potted flowers and vegetable peelings from the kitchen were thrown, into a tangled mass that gradually changed color and broke down until eventually it was tipped out onto the soil as dark-brown compost, still teeming with skinny red worms that wriggled frantically in the light.

I think of the wood-burning stove that we had installed in the house. I think of the heat and the logs that quickly turned to ashes. The stack of wood under the stove which, after a few hours, had dwindled to a point where it needed to be replenished. In the winter it was my job to bring in the wood, just a single bundle in the late afternoon after school. Logs that sent heat out into the room as they burned down and turned to powder.

It is all this dissolution that has formed a core, a family with set places; that has given rise to traditions and a place to come back to, and I think of those foggy days with Thomas, as if it is the dissolution that holds things together.

But now I am on a train and my parents are probably going around the house as if nothing had happened. I left the house in darkness, with only the flashlight and the street lamps to light my way. It was chilly, but not a winter chill, and I walked through the residential streets, past suburban shops, down main roads and into town, where at last I boarded a bus that took me to Bruxelles-Midi.

At the station I went into the only café that was open. It was almost empty when I got there but over the next few hours I saw the station slowly fill with travelers while I changed my seat every now and again and waited for a solution, a way out, a journey that made sense, but the only solution I could think of was to go north. I had to have winter, so around midmorning, once the stream of travelers had tailed off, I bought a ticket for a train that would take me north.

I no longer listen to conversations on the train because I know where I am going and no one says *Winterreise*, even though we crossed the German border a while ago.

#405

I got off the train at Cologne because it was the last stop and after stepping off I walked through the station and out onto a square. To one side of me the cathedral reared up and as I came out the cathedral clock began to chime. It was four o'clock and, oddly enough, even warmer than in Brussels, and on the square in front of the cathedral I was met by a mild breeze. It was an afternoon with no rain, quite warm for November. Far too warm for winter anyway. Halfway across the square I stopped short, turned around, strode back to the station and took the first train going north. It was bound for Bremen and when I got to Bremen station I walked into town and found the hotel where I had stayed after delivering my forlorn young friend to the lady in beige.

I asked for the same room as before. It was late and I was too tired to go out and get something to eat, too tired to think about my parents, who were no doubt sitting across from one another in the kitchen, in the corner, with my place at the table squashed up against the wall, possibly with a bowl of quinces on the table and the scent of November in the air.

Instead I ate the remains of our Christmas pudding, a rather gooey dinner, but there was something comforting about the taste, the taste of care and tenderness perhaps, as if there was still someone who worried about me, a heavy taste of Christmas and family and years gone by.

As I was brushing my teeth, I caught sight of myself in the makeup mirror in the bathroom, tired and bound for winter. It was a double-sided mirror and as I stood there lost in thought I happened to flip it over. A moment later I glanced up and found myself looking at a magnified face, still mine, but not only larger, older too, because on closer inspection there were wrinkles and small blemishes I had never noticed before. It felt like a leap. From child to adult almost. Having a family is aging. Lullabies and Christmas carols give you wrinkles.

Before I went to sleep I took off the dress I had on top but kept my new dress on all night. This morning I woke up early because it was far too warm to sleep in wool, but the dress has stayed with me, and my woolen underwear, which I had laid beside me on the bed, is still here too. I am ready for winter and after breakfast I began to plan my journey north.

I had come to the conclusion that I would have to go to Norway, find a ferry that would sail me up the coast and carry me to a place with snow and I spent most of the day checking ferry routes. Initially one from Kiel, but that had no sailings on the eighteenth of November. I could have left on the nineteenth, but I can't wait for that. From Denmark there were two ferries, a fast one and a slow one. The slow one was an overnight ferry. But what would happen if I sailed through the night? Could a ferry sail through the eighteenth of November? Would the day turn into the nineteenth? Would the ship go back to its point of departure? And would I go with it? It is a tricky question and at the travel agency where I inquired all they could tell me was that there was a ferry leaving at 6:30 p.m. I could make that if I took the eleven o'clock train, then I would be in Norway in the morning. Of the nineteenth. In principle. There was in fact another ferry, a high-speed ferry, but on this particular day it had been canceled. There had recently been a storm in Norway and the ferry had been damaged, otherwise it would have got me to Norway before midnight. I was offered the choice of several flights, but I do not trust the aircraft of the eighteenth of November, or aircraft in general, and I do not drive, so I decided to take the train instead. I could take it to Denmark and carry on north from there. It would be slower, but not difficult so tomorrow morning I will take the train north. I am sitting at the window in my hotel room, it is afternoon, the sky is overcast and I am on my way to winter. I look down the street, the station is close by, I can see it if I open the window and stick my head out. I can look out on the square across the street, where lights are being hung in the trees. The trams roll past and I hear their sounds, their acceleration and their stopping, I can see a gray sky and I feel a chill in the air, different from that rainy day in Clairon, different from that cool November day in Paris, different from autumn in Brussels, because there is no wind, different from the excessively mild afternoon in Cologne, there is a nip in the air, a sign perhaps that winter is coming.

But why don't I go somewhere warmer? To Spain or Italy, to a Greek island, to a quiet beach? I should be wishing for sunshine and summer after so many days of rain, but what I want is winter.

I want December and January. I want a year that will start moving. I want the cold and dark of winter, not just a single day of showers and chilly sunlight, not just mild days with rain and more rain, not just gray skies and a nip in the air.

#406

There is not much winter to be had here and no snow at all. It is afternoon. The weather is gray and still and not particularly cold. Immediately after breakfast this morning I took a train from Bremen to Hamburg. I traveled through the north German countryside, which was barely discernible through the morning mist. The skies were clear over Neumünster but not long afterward we ran into a dense fog that left only a few gnarled and almost bare trees looming alongside the railway line. Before long, though, the fog lifted completely and now I am in Denmark, in Odense. I have been here before, some years ago, to attend an auction with Thomas, and we sat here, right where I am sitting now, in a café in the farthest corner of the station. We were passing the time, waiting for our train, and now here I am, passing the time, waiting for my train. It must have been winter when we were here, but I don't remember exactly when. It might also have been early spring. All I remember is that it started snowing. We had several suitcases sitting around us, because we had bought books at the auction. This was in the early days, during T. & T. Selter's first year. We often went to auctions together, returning home with bags and suitcases full of books, not to Clairon, but to Brussels, where our business consisted of some bookcases and a desk in the corner of my minuscule apartment, into which Thomas had moved, along with the beginnings of T. & T. Selter. We had been lucky with a few deals, we had discovered our own special feel for antiquarian books. I had gradually developed a unique sense—that is how it felt anyway, like a sense—or a certain instinct at any rate for the books, for the typography, the paper and the scientific plates, and it turned out that we had a knack for finding the right books, that we could find buyers, or rather: Thomas could find the buyers, who soon realized we were able to track down works that they wanted or that they didn't even know they wanted. We were keen, we attended auctions, we lugged suitcases and bags, and we knew that it was the two of us, that we were in this together, that it was our joint efforts that made it work, we were a company, traveling and loving, buying and selling, we made interesting finds and occasional bad buys that took a while to sell, but that was all right, because we were together on the mistakes, no matter which of us had made them, just as we were together on the lucky finds.

At the station we had found the café where I now sit in an armchair with my papers in front of me. We had deposited ourselves on a sofa with our luggage around us, with coffee cups and a cake or a sandwich or whatever we had in front of us. With plenty of time to spare before our train was due we had got up to go down to the platforms, which were on the level below the café area and could be seen from the station's large panoramic windows, and as we made our way out, lugging and dragging our bags and baggage, snow began to fall on the tracks and on the platforms where our train would soon be pulling in

The snow fell heavily, in large flakes that swirled this way and that, hesitantly, due to their size. Our train hadn't yet arrived so we stood at the window, watching the huge snowflakes drifting down onto roofs and railway tracks. Other travelers had also gathered by the windows and we all stood there, watching the snow falling outside and landing on the platform canopies, on the empty tracks and doubtless on the streets around the station, on buildings and roads we could not see due to the density of the snow that had filled the air. We stood there as if inside a container made of glass, but not one of those souvenir globes in which snow falls over a city or a building when it is shaken, because here it was the other way around: it was the world outside that had been shaken, while we remained still and the snow fell and fell outside the station, which had suddenly been transformed from an ordinary railway station to an attraction, a magical scene.

Shortly afterward, when we emerged, the snow had stopped, but everything was covered in a blanket of white: we traveled on the train through all the whiteness, which soon vanished again, either because the snow had melted or because we had come to places where no snow had fallen, I don't know, because by then we weren't paying so much attention to the landscape. Once settled on the half-empty train, with a table between us, we had taken some of our purchases out of our bags. I remember leafing through a small booklet, *De Analysi aquarum frigidarum*, and I also recall a copy of *Traité des affinités chymiques*, translated from Latin to French, but both by a Swedish writer, Bergman or Bergson, I think. It may be that I remember these books because they were among our bad buys and proved nearly impossible to sell. It took several years for us to sell the first of these works, and the second was never sold, probably because I had not noticed that it was missing a couple of plates which ought to have been attached at the back of the book. In the end we gave it to Lisa as a Christmas present, after she started studying chemistry. I don't remember the titles of the other books we had bought, but I remember them as volumes discovered in swirls of snow.

That is probably why I have come here. I had been thinking of winter, but there is no snow today and no winter in sight, unless the candles on the tables are trying to show the way to winter. There is too much November in the air. There is November in the soft armchair to which I have retreated, away from the trails of travelers, and where I sit juggling my sheets of white paper and writing about snow, because I still haven't started using my green clothbound notebook. I write without lines and without direction on a little pile of paper, with a folder for support, even though the notebook would be more manageable in armchairs, at café tables and on train seats. Nonetheless, I go on writing, conscious that my loose sheets of paper may contain my last hope that this fault in time is only temporary, the hope that the next sheet will never be filled, because time will return to normal and there will be no more eighteenths of November to write about.

I no longer believe that time will suddenly return to normal, of course, but I still have to allow for that possibility. The moment I write the first line in the notebook I will have given my November days permission to continue, line after line, page after page, until the book is full of eighteenths of November. That's a lot of pages, a lot of lines, and I can't think so far ahead. I want to escape from November and into a world with seasons. I want snow and rime on the grass, perhaps a few days of hard frost, not necessarily an arctic winter or deep snow drifts, simply winter as I know it: chilly days and gardens with dry seed heads and a haze of white, nights with cold, starry skies that may on rare occasions bring snow. I want January blasts and frost. I want puddles covered by thin films of ice that crack when you step on them. And gales. Winter gales. Frosty wind. And snow like the snow that falls on old Selter's garden, enough to cover the leeks with a thin layer of white and the Swiss chard to grow soft, with tender, crinkly hearts that will grow no further until the frost is gone. And the spring that follows. I want cool spring breezes and milder winds. I want March and April and a low spring sun. I want soft sunlight and Easter days. I want May and warm air. I want June and July and August, but only if they come after winter and spring. I want summer and the seashore. I want days of blazing sunshine and balmy evenings. Evenings when you can sit outside at midnight and listen to the darkness. I want late summer and early autumn, I want the morning mists of September, October's clear skies and falling leaves, because time has passed. I want the seasons to be set right, for them to be dependable, for them to move with long, slow strides back into their proper order.

I don't know why I didn't check the weather forecast before I got off the train, because I should have known that there would be no winter only a few hours further north, and now I am sitting in my armchair in a corner of the station, thinking of winter, but I have to move on, this is not where I will find winter. I find railway-station sounds: loudspeaker announcements, the hiss of coffee machines, the chink of cups, the faint sound of a train stopping. I sit here with a view of travelers, of coats too thin for winter, of scarves tied too loosely, of light backpacks and shoulder bags, and all around me is November, but in a moment I will go out to find a train going north. I have bought a ticket to Copenhagen, where I will change to a train to Malmö and then I will be in Sweden, and then I will surely be on my way to winter. On my way to something resembling December, something that can show me the way to January. And to February. I hope.

#407

It was on the way to the train that things went wrong. I hadn't even got as far as the platform. I had just got to my feet, had scarcely made it out of my corner in the café before I slipped up. Not because I hadn't noticed the difference in height: a step down to the station concourse from the secluded area where I had been sitting. It probably had more to do with the fact that I had hoisted my bag over my shoulder, thereby shifting my center of gravity, just as I stepped down onto the concourse floor, or thought that I was stepping onto the concourse floor, because I landed wrongly, caught my foot on the edge of the step, my leg buckled under me, I was thrown off balance, went over on my foot, spun around and fell, bag and all, onto the stone floor. I didn't hurt myself very much in the fall, but when I picked myself up I discovered that I had twisted my ankle so badly that I couldn't put any weight on it. A couple of passersby helped me onto my feet and parked me next to a high table on which I could lean. I assured them that I was fine, that they were not to worry.

After a few minutes to collect myself I was able to put enough weight on my foot to hobble over to the descent to Platform

4, from which my train was due to leave. Fortunately, I was in good time and through the window I could see that my train had not yet arrived. I crossed to the escalator and took it down to the platform, where my train was just pulling in.

There was still plenty of time till departure and I limped along the side of the train looking for my carriage. I managed to locate it, haul both my foot and my bag on board and find my seat before the train set off. The seat next to mine was empty so I arranged myself with my back to the window, removed the boot from my injured foot and rested it on the empty seat.

Over the next hour my ankle swelled so much that I had to give up trying to put my boot on again as we approached Copenhagen. It hurt so much that all notion of carrying on to Sweden had fled. I took the escalator up to the station concourse and at the information desk I was given directions to a pharmacy where I would be able to buy a bandage and possibly some painkillers, and to a hotel where I could spend the night.

At the pharmacy, which, luckily for me, was near the station, I bought painkillers and an elastic bandage for my foot, but was also advised to see a doctor because, judging by the size of it, my ankle might be more than just twisted. It might be broken, or I might have torn a ligament, the assistant at the pharmacy warned me as I attempted to pay for my purchases while standing on one leg, with my boot in my hand. In any event it would probably be a good idea to rest the foot and preferably to keep it raised, on a couple of cushions for example. She gave me the phone number for the on-call doctor and the address of an emergency room.

Sitting on a low bench in the pharmacy I wrapped the bandage around my foot, then I went out onto the street and soon found the hotel, which was only a few minutes' walk away. I crossed a wide road, located the hotel entrance, went inside and up to the reception desk, still clutching my boot, but now with a bandage around my foot providing an explanation for this. I was in luck, they had some vacant rooms and having yet again explained my problem with cleaning products, I was handed the key card for a room that had not been occupied for a couple of days due to some minor water damage to the ceiling. I took the elevator up to my room, swallowed two painkillers, lay down on the bed with my foot on a pillow and gazed at the water damage, a dark patch in a corner of the ceiling.

I didn't get much sleep last night and I didn't go down for breakfast this morning. The pain, which had receded slightly yesterday evening, returned during the night and even though I have taken a couple of the painkillers from the pharmacist, I don't think there is any way around it, I will have to go to the emergency room. Winter has not come and I have not come north, or rather: not far enough north, and now I am sitting waiting for the pills to take effect. I slept in my woolen dress, but that doesn't make it winter. It is warm here and in a little while I will take off this dress, get the old one out of my bag and go to the emergency room.

* * *

I had to wait a while, but not as long as the hotel receptionist had predicted, and now I am back in my hotel room, complete with a new bandage and some useful information.

I took a taxi to the emergency room, spent a couple of hours in the waiting room and, after a brief exam, sat in a long corridor, waiting to be taken in for an X-ray. The doctor didn't think my foot was broken, but said it should be checked, to be on the safe side.

On one of the other chairs in the long corridor sat a woman of about my own age or possibly a little older, with a child who had hurt himself. The woman's cargo bike had tipped over when she braked for a red light, her son had fallen out of the box at the front and his hand had been caught under it. He had screamed loudly, louder than she had ever heard him scream in all his five years. He has never cried much, she said, but this time he had and she was afraid he might have broken his hand so she had cycled straight to the emergency room, which was not far away and now they were sitting there, like me, waiting to have an X-ray taken. The boy had stopped crying, but his hand was swollen, so we sat there with our respective injuries, swapping experiences. The boy spoke English, having attended an international kindergarten when his mother was studying in the Netherlands and he had suddenly become very interested in my sore ankle. Did I cry when it happened? Why hadn't I gone straight to the emergency room when I hurt myself? And had I really sat with my foot up on a train seat? He looked at his mother, who clearly did not allow children to put their feet on seats. I assured him that I had taken my boot off first and his mother nodded approvingly. She was a meteorologist and had been taking her son to kindergarten before going to work at the Meteorological Institute when the accident happened.

We chatted a bit about the weather and my quest for colder days and to my own surprise I found myself telling her that I worked for a movie company and that I was out scouting for possible locations for a production to be shot in November next year which would feature scenes from different seasons. The autumn scenes would be shot in Flanders, I said, but I was now going north to find locations for the winter scenes. They had to be places with a reasonable chance of snow in November.

To my astonishment she believed my story and since we were just sitting waiting anyway she took her laptop out of her bag and began to look for snow. She found a couple of spots in Sweden and Norway and a few minutes later when her son was called in to be X-rayed she asked me to wait till she got back. Not long afterward I too was called in and had my foot X-rayed. Nothing was broken but my ankle was badly sprained. I should expect it to take several weeks to heal and there wasn't much I could do except rest it as much as possible. A fresh bandage was applied to the foot and a plastic boot over the bandage so that I could get about outside even without a shoe.

The meteorologist's son had not broken anything either and since she had already let her office know that she wouldn't be coming in to work that day due to the accident she suggested that we find a café and take a closer look at my seasons. She had promised her son an ice cream. I said I was sure that could be arranged and suggested that I take them to lunch.

Shortly afterward we were sitting in a café with coffee, sandwiches and ice cream for the meteorologist's son. Once we had finished our sandwiches and the meteorologist had also eaten half of her son's ice cream she began to check snowfall distribution in Scandinavia and the statistics for snow in November. She showed me a number of websites I could explore myself later. If I had a memory stick she could transfer everything she had found to that and I could take it from there. I didn't have a memory stick, I said, but I could go out and buy one and maybe I could take her son with me. I had seen a toy shop on the way to the café and I thought we might find a present for him while she was working.

The boy was all for a trip to the toy shop, he slipped his good hand into mine without hesitation and informed his mother that we were going to look at toys. She agreed, a little doubtfully, and we left the café and walked down the street to the little toy shop, me limping along, him with his bandaged hand.

On the way there we talked about kindergartens and he told me in his child's English about the differences between his Dutch and Danish kindergartens. I told him about my Belgian kindergarten and then we talked about how the word 'kindergarten' was actually a German word meaning 'children's garden.' Soon we were deep in conversation about children's gardens and gardens for children and why a nursery school could be called a garden.

After a look around the toy shop the boy surprised me by choosing a red watering can with white dots rather than one of the many boxes of building blocks or plastic action figures. I added a small trowel and a four-pack of vegetable seeds which the assistant sales clerk slipped into a shopping bag for him, and after a visit to a electronics store a little farther down the street we returned to the café. I now had my memory stick and had briefly considered whether I should also buy a laptop, but it probably wouldn't have been able to retain its data so I abandoned that idea.

Shortly afterward, when we walked back into the café, the meteorologist's son—carrying his toy shop bag very carefully in his bandaged hand and the watering can in the other—glanced at his mother as if unsure what she would say about this present. She was particularly happy to see that he could use both hands without any pain and she smiled at the sight of the watering can. She told me that they were currently creating a communal kitchen garden in the backyard of the building where they lived.

I handed her the memory stick and she gave me a rundown on the temperature graphs and files she had come up with. She had found several places where there had been snow in November every year for the past five years. Generally, you had to go quite far north to be sure of snow, but at the moment they actually had some in the south of Sweden. That very morning there had been snow on the ground in Lund, some miles inland. An inch, she said, but the temperature had risen since then, so it would have melted by the end of the day. And Stockholm had had rain, then clear skies and frost at night. This was not unusual, but it was not something I could count on either. If I wanted to be sure of frost and snow I would have to go farther north, but from a purely meteorological point of view there should be no problem in finding suitable locations.

She had also looked at spring and summer weather conditions. She had found statistics for various areas and some minute-by-minute weather charts. There were plenty of possibilities. For spring scenes she had selected places that tended to get a lot of rain and should therefore not be too dry, but whether any of them would be damp enough to give the illusion of spring she couldn't say. One could, of course, travel to the southern hemisphere. There one might have spring in November. The south of England was a more obvious option. She herself had been in Cornwall on vacation, where the autumn weather was so warm that sheep farmers had started bringing their lambs into the world in midautumn instead of having the spring lambs which Nature preferred to produce. There was an almost springlike air to the fields, with all the newborn lambs, she said.

Summer weather was to be found in several places down south. She had identified some spots which had what northern Europeans would regard as typical summer weather: quite warm, with bright sunshine, the occasional cloud and a water temperature of around sixty-six. She had pinpointed a couple of areas in southern Spain which she thought would fit the bill. The current forecast was for mild nights and windless evenings and she was pretty sure it would be possible to find some summery locations.

She couldn't guarantee that next year's weather would follow the statistical pattern, but it would at least act as a guideline. I thanked her. She had no idea what a big help this was, I said, and I told her a little bit about the film. I said that the narrative stretched over a year, from autumn to autumn, and told the story of a man who had been left alone when his wife died but had gone on growing as many vegetables as when she was alive. The film dealt with the people he met in his efforts to give away the surplus produce from his garden. We needed to use gardens from all four seasons but had only a couple of weeks in which to shoot the outdoor scenes, so we would have to move with the weather. The meteorologist wanted to know whether we would be showing vegetables at different stages of growth at our locations and how we would solve that problem. I said that we hadn't decided yet, but we could probably get hold of some of the vegetables and plant them out when we were ready to shoot the scenes. I have no idea where my lies came from. I have never been in the habit of lying, but here I was, constructing a movie that did not exist.

Fortunately, the meteorologist then began to reflect on our strange relationship with the seasons. She talked about astronomical seasons and meteorological seasons. About the calendar year's division into spring and summer months, about people's surprise when meteorological phenomena did not accord with the calendar, even though everyone knew that any attempt to synchronize the weather with the predictability of planets and calendars was pointless.

She did not believe, however, that the seasons could be regarded as meteorological phenomena. Temperature and precipitation were meteorological phenomena, she said. Cold and heat, cloudbursts and drought. But seasons? She saw them more as psychological phenomena. Memory concentrates. Accepted stereotypes. Conglomerates of experiences and feelings, perhaps. People ask if it won't soon be summer, even though we are well into July, simply because the summer has been on the cool side. As a meteorologist one is almost expected to deliver particular weather conditions at particular times of year, she said. A proper summer. A proper winter. As if you hadn't done your job until you had delivered a certain sort of weather. Aren't we going to have a winter this year? As if the seasons were a concept of sorts that we dragged around with us. From childhood perhaps, she said, with winter snow and summer sun. Or perhaps not even that. Perhaps the human seasons really only existed in films or in our photo albums. Especially if you have children. She did it herself: took pictures of typical seasons. She had noticed that she took more pictures when the seasons lived up to our expectations of them: pictures of snow in winter and bright sunshine in summer, a hot day on the beach, red and yellow leaves and a child in rain boots in autumn—and always snaps with sandals in summer, even in summers when most days were rain boot days. As if we had templates for the seasons and when everything fits we take a picture. As if it is an event in itself that the weather has got it right. If it is winter in a film there is always a little snow, she said. Or frost. Even if the film is set in southern Europe there will be a sprinkling of white, to let us know that it is winter.

I, too, only needed a little snow. A sprinkling of white. Just enough that it would no longer be autumn. Some wizened flower heads covered with snow or frost would be fine. A bare tree silhouetted against the evening sky. A few rows of leeks sprinkled with white and possibly a greenhouse with snow on the roof. Puddles covered by a thin film of ice that cracks when you step on it, I said.

This seemed to amuse her. She looked at the boy, who had climbed up onto her lap and opened the box containing the packets of seeds. We talked of spring and greening fields. But in actual fact, she said, most fields are sown in the autumn, the seeds sprout and the fields green up then, and yet we equate autumn with brown fields and all the green growth with spring.

I told them that some of the seeds in the boy's packets could be sown now. If they sowed cauliflower seeds in pots in the autumn the seedlings could then be planted out to give them early

cauliflower. If they were lucky they would be able to pick cauliflower before the caterpillars hatched out and ate them all. If
she had a balcony the plants could sit out there once they had
sprouted or she could put them out in the backyard and cover
them in the winter if the weather was too cold. I could hear myself passing on one of Thomas's grandfather's gardening tips
here. He had always sown his cauliflower in the autumn. That
didn't sound right to the meteorologist. Yes, really, I said, you
can. It occurred to me that it must be about as warm in Copenhagen now as it had been in Clairon when old Selter was young,
although November might be a little late. The sowing of cauliflower in the autumn was entered on his gardening scheme in
the shed and Thomas and I had seen him inspecting his covered
plant pots during the winter, but we had not yet tried doing it
ourselves. It's hard to sow seeds when Nature is closing down.

After we had exchanged a few remarks on gardens and seedlings and a balcony that she would use for growing cauliflower,
the meteorologist handed me my memory stick and prepared to
leave. She helped her son to slip his bandaged hand into the arm
of his coat. She was clearly relieved that he had not been more
badly hurt and said she hoped my foot would be better soon. A
minute later, out on the street, we said goodbye and I thanked
her again for her help and reminded her to drive carefully. They
didn't have far to go, in fact we were standing at the intersection
where the accident had happened and they lived just a little farther down the street, she told me, before showing me the way to
a bus stop where I could catch a bus into the city center.

While waiting for the bus I caught a faint whiff of winter. It
wasn't raining, but the air was damp. Without my wool dress

and with one foot covered only by a bandage and a plastic boot I felt cold. As I boarded the bus it occurred to me that the weather here was possibly more like a December day in Brussels or Clairon after all. It was growing dark and I already felt that my meteorologist friend had shown me the way to winter.

Back in my hotel room I took my memory stick out of my bag. My faith in the technology of the eighteenth of November is minimal and I entertain no great hope that there will be any data on the memory stick tomorrow. Fortunately, there is a computer in the hotel lobby and in a little while I will take my green notebook downstairs, access the information I need from the memory stick and write it down. Not for a film, but for the seasons that lie waiting for me somewhere in the eighteenth of November.

#408

When I got up this morning and went down to the lobby I found that, sure enough, there was nothing on the memory stick. I had spent most of the evening at the hotel computer and had copied all the key information into my green notebook. At reception I had been able to get printouts of temperature graphs and snowfall tables which I folded and slipped into the notebook. To be on the safe side I slept with all of this, including the memory stick, under my pillow. The stick was still there when I woke up but it proved to be empty. As expected, the notebook was also still there, full of notes and jottings and with folded printouts of tables and graphs tucked in at the back.

My foot was still swollen and tender and I had breakfast with a boot on one foot and the bandage on the other. When I was finished I went back to my room, removed the bandage and limped down to the nearest shoe shop, where I bought a pair of thick socks and a pair of boots one size too large. The boots have both zippers and laces and with a woolen sock on the one foot and the other boot left unzipped they just fit. So now I am ready for winter. I walk slowly, hobbling along, but not feeling cold or wet, and tomorrow I will carry on northward.

#409

When I woke this morning the swelling had gone down a little and now I can zip up my boot. I walk slowly, I walk with my bootlaces loosely tied, but I am walking toward winter and after I had packed my bag and left my old boots in the hotel closet I made my way haltingly to the station, where I bought a ticket to Lund.

I have already secured a vacant hotel room, having spoken to the receptionist at just after five this morning and asked for help to reserve a room at a hotel in Lund with a check-in time of seven a.m. Then, at just after seven, I asked the newly arrived morning receptionist for help to delay my Lund check-in until midmorning, so I can now be doubly sure that my room will not be occupied when I wake up on the eighteenth of November.

The meteorologist had spoken of snow in the morning, but when I arrived a little before noon the snow was almost gone.

That's all right, though, because I can feel a nip in the air, it is winter air, and tomorrow morning I expect snow again. I have picked my way through wet streets and I have seen small patches of snow in a park. I have thought of December and January. If I count the days I come to the thirty-first of December.

I am sitting in a room with a view of snowless roofs, but I am waiting for snow. I am waiting for winter. Patiently, because I know it is coming. In my green notebook I have written *December 31st*, it may be a lie, a white lie, a winter lie, but I only write it here, on a sheet of paper, and in a little while I will go out to buy a bottle of champagne and I will celebrate my little white lies and hope for a new year with winter and spring and summer.

#410

I woke to snow. I saw it as soon as I opened my eyes: white, almost bluish, light fell through the window and the roofs outside my window were covered with snow. My room is on the fourth floor of a small hotel in the center of town and I could see the snow from my bed because I had not closed the curtains. I got up to fetch my notebook, slipped back under the duvet and wrote *January 1st*. I wrote *snow* and *winter*. I wrote *Sweden* and *Lund*, the address of my hotel and my room number. I wrote that there was snow on the roofs and later, after I had been out in the town, I wrote about the cold and the wet streets on which the snow was melting as I wandered slowly around in my slightly too big boots, which I had kept in a bag at the foot of my bed during the night. I didn't write that they had been in a bag, but I wrote about where one can buy gloves and that there is a café where one can get hot mulled wine.

I have found my way to winter. It is a new life. A life with seasons. It is not a truer year, moving in the depths under my day. It is a year that runs parallel to my eighteenth of November. I know that I am building something. A construction. A jigsaw puzzle, which I am putting together from the pieces I can find. But I don't write this in my green notebook. I write about all the things that make my days winter days and there are enough pages in the notebook to write about winter and spring and summer and autumn. I no longer believe that I will suddenly wake up to a time that has returned to normal. But I believe in seasons. Slender, homemade. It is not the eighteenth of November when I have my green notebook. Or, at least, not only the eighteenth of November. It is also New Year's Day. It was Christmas. There was a bird and roast potatoes and Bûche de Noël and Christmas pudding, and now it is New Year's Day and yesterday evening was New Year's Eve. It wasn't easy to get hold of champagne on a November evening but I did and in my green notebook I have written the name of a restaurant that sells champagne to go, because I couldn't find a shop that sold champagne, and I have written *nyårsafton*, because that is what New Year's Eve is called in Swedish.

#416

I am gaining on the year. I find places that remind me of January. Of the month of January as I know it. January in Clairon and January in Belgium and January in northern Europe. I don't need much snow. A sprinkling. And that I have already had. I find January in the shops. I find January dishes. I eat soup, or I drink apple and cinnamon tea.

Suddenly I see that this is how my life will be, year after year. That my seasons book is my manual, my traveling companion, my guide. That what I am building is my future. If I am to have a future I must have years, and if I am to have years, I must have seasons. Without seasons, no time. If I want seasons, I will have to build them myself. If I am to have a future, I will have to build it myself. I put the pieces together, little fragments of season and I write it all down in my manual: the ingredients of the seasons.

It is not like a garden. I sow nothing, I do not water, I do not harvest. It is not like a house. I do not fell trees, I do not break stone, I do not fire tiles, I build no walls, I do not lay shingles. I find ready-made elements, small parts for season building, I amass information in my green book, I think of tools, of screwdrivers, Allen wrenches and nuts and bolts of various sizes, I think of screws and nails, of glue and cement, I assemble the parts and maybe I can build a year.

And if it works I will have a seasons machine, that is what I am building. I see myself circulating through these seasons, returning to them, that I will have need of winter again, and of spring. I see myself having to create my own summers, that I am working my way toward a template, a pattern by which to live. I am filled with a strange excitement. There is something to look forward to: to the spring that I will build myself. But first I must have winter. Things have to fit. And in the spring I can look forward to summer.

#424

I am still traveling north. Toward the cold and toward February. I fill my seasons book with information. I find snow. Not much, but it is cold here, and there is more to winter than snow. Stockholm in November is winter. There is no snow here as there was in Lund, even though I am now farther north, but it rained during the night, the rain was followed by frost and if I get up early I can find parks with paths running through them and on the paths there are puddles and on some of the puddles the cold has left a thin film of ice. I can put my foot through the ice with a faint crack, I can stroll through grass, making soft, frosty sounds and I walk with careful tread across a lawn in my slightly too large boots.

My foot still aches, but the swelling has gone down and now I wear thick woolen socks on both feet, because wool goes with winter. Winter goes with wool. Winter goes with big boots and I have found winter for my boots. They walk through the park, they walk through winter puddles and they let me walk with them as best I can.

When I am not walking through morning frost, in winter boots, through frozen puddles, I go to winter cinemas and read winter books. I have found a library that has English books, I have found bookshops selling winter stories and sometimes I come across films with winter titles and I sit in the winter gloom in my winter boots for a couple of hours, then I go back outside and it is still winter.

I write everything down in my seasons book. I write the titles of books and films. I write the names of hotels and the numbers of vacant rooms. I write words in the language of winter, I tell myself that I could learn Swedish, that I will come back again and again, that I will need to speak Winter and I have discovered that in Swedish the Milky Way is called the winter street, *Vintergatan*. It is called that all year round. Also in November, but I do not write November in my seasons book. I write November on sheets of white paper that I will put back into my bag in a moment. There they will lie together with other November papers, enclosed within a black cardboard folder and outside of that folder it is winter.

#427

What do I miss? Lighting a fire in the fireplace in a living room. So I find a living room with a fireplace and logs and matches and I light a fire.

What do I miss? I miss a winter with a thin layer of snow in a garden with leeks and Swiss chard. So I find a garden. I find an empty house. I find duvets and blankets and in the morning I can look out on a garden covered in a thin layer of snow.

What do I miss? Sometimes I miss spring, but it is not yet time for that. I must wait. I have left my old coat, which was far too light, on a kitchen countertop in a wooden house where I stayed for a couple of days and have bought a warm winter coat instead, because I now have winter. Proper winter. Thanks, meteorologist.

#446

Now I cannot get enough of winter. It is not enough that it resembles winter as I know it. I cannot content myself with snow that doesn't last, a light sprinkling. I am searching for the heart of winter, consummate winter, concentrated winter. I travel through mountains, I move upward, northward and along narrow roads where the snow has already settled as if it means to stay. I gaze at the landscape and write names in my notebook. Place after place. Name after name. I make a note of streets and restaurants. I write the addresses of empty houses and recipes for winter dishes in my book.

#451

These are quiet winter days. I wake to silence. I have winter now, I am in Finland and I have gone into hibernation. I have traveled north, and I think *Siberian cold*, although I don't know why the cold here should be *Siberian*, it is Finnish, and I find dictionaries and try to learn new winter languages in my house, where no one lives and it is cold, and I slide down under duvets and blankets and stay still. *Peitot ja viltit*. Duvets and blankets. *Talvi ja lumi*. Winter and snow.

I see myself returning here year after year, hibernating here, and each year I will pick up more words. I will find words for pillows and sheets and other bed linen, for beds and chairs, for kitchens with all of their contents: plates and knives and forks and pots, I will find words for the houses, for roofs and chimneys, I will introduce doors and windows to my winter language, I will add forests and roads and towns, new words every year, a language that grows and grows in cold and snow, and winter will come, and spring and summer and autumn again, and I will come back and find more words. Something is growing. I am starting to imagine a future. Thanks, winter language.

#456

I eat winter food and buy winter clothes. I move from place to place, slowly, but not too slowly, I never stay too long because if I do, I can tell that my language is not the only thing that is growing. A monster is also growing. It is not something I write about in my seasons book. That I am devouring my world. That I have to move on, to avoid eating up my world. That I am a monster on the move, a winter monster.

I have seen a winter soup erased from a menu board in a restaurant because I had had soup there several days in a row. I have seen empty spaces in a supermarket where I have taken jars of herring, rye bread, packages of cheese. I find other places, I change my winter habits, I switch to brown bread because there is loads of that in the shops, I find different cheeses and larger shops where it is impossible to tell that I have been there. I forage my way through February, I have gone north, I travel on,

I travel by bus and by train. I move. Slowly but surely through winter.

The days grow shorter the farther north I go. I wake in the morning, I go through my winter day and before I know it the day is over.

#462

I may have traveled too far into winter. I am in Norway. I had taken the train and came to a small town, but the local hotel was closed and I did not feel like going looking for empty houses. In a little café in the town center I was served hot tea and broccoli pie by an apron-clad older man with a gray beard who informed me that there was a guest house outside of town, about twenty minutes away, where I might get a bed for the night. He offered to call and check whether they had any vacancies. They did, and when I had finished my meal he phoned for a taxi. The driver was a friendly woman who spoke English and almost fluent French, having spent two years in Toulouse when she was young.

We drove out of the town which, after only a couple of minutes, had thinned out to just a scattering of houses, then onto the highway. We talked mainly about the weather. About the winters, which had become milder and the storms, which had become more severe. A particularly fierce storm had recently brought down trees in the area my driver told me. She pointed to the passing countryside, where a number of trees lay on the ground with their roots exposed. I told her that there had also been a storm in the north of France, not as bad, but a tremendous amount of rain had fallen, there had been a risk of flooding and in Clairon-sous-Bois where I lived, I said, we had in the past had flooding on the low-lying ground alongside the river.

After the storm they had had snow, the driver told me. Luckily, though, they had managed to clear away the fallen trees before that, otherwise it would have been hard for the snowplows to get through. The road was not very wide, but it had been cleared and there was room for the traffic and for the snow piled up along the shoulder. We drove past a forest that occasionally gave way to a stretch of rocky wall, then another stretch of forest. Running along the other side of the road was a crash barrier and beyond the crash barrier I caught sporadic glimpses of a steep slope. The road ran pretty straight for most of the journey and it was only when we came to a bend that I had a sense of being high up.

We must have been about halfway and going pretty fast. My driver obviously knew the area well and I think she wanted to drop me off and get back to town as quickly as possible. I had the feeling that she had other customers waiting in town and that she had delayed a planned pickup to drive me to the guest house. I suspect that her taxi is the only one in the area. At any rate, we were speeding along, chatting about France and Belgium, partly in English but mostly in French. I had fastened my seat belt and sat in the back with my bag beside me, glancing about me a bit apprehensively because I have never been keen on traveling by car and have no great need for speed.

We had passed some cars, not many, but the road was not exactly deserted. We met trucks and sedan cars and one semitrailer with a load of timber. The highway was dotted with white patches of snow, firm and smooth, mostly on our side of the road, there was a little bump every time we drove over one, but this did not prompt my driver to slow down at all, not even when a truck appeared up ahead, big and blue, coming toward us on a straight stretch, with a long tail of cars behind it.

Suddenly, as we were passing a wall of rock on our right, we ran into larger patches of snow and just as we were about to draw level with the truck the taxi went into a skid, we veered off course and there came a shriek from the front seat at the same moment that the driver jammed on the brakes, a scream, or cry, I suppose, that came from the pit of her stomach, deep and full of fear. Our car began to shudder and shake as it slewed back and forth and I felt nothing but horror as we jumped and bumped over the rutted stretch of ice and snow and asphalt, out of control and in constant danger of swerving straight into the blue truck a few yards ahead of us.

My driver had clearly lost control of her vehicle, which was sliding all over the road. The truck drew closer and closer until it was looming over us in all its massive blue bulk, while we bounced and rattled about in a car that threatened, at any second, to take us straight into its path. And then, suddenly, it was past us, the truck, and right behind it the string of cars, rolling by outside one by one while our car carried on, in its own lane, still shuddering, but staying on the right side of the road. The whole thing cannot have lasted more than a few seconds and although I don't know how it could be, I'm sure I saw the faces of the other drivers and that I saw terror in the eyes behind the windows of all those cars as we passed each other. It must have been quite obvious that our car was out of control, either that or I am only imagining the expressions on those faces.

By the time the truck and the line of cars had passed us we had solid ground under our wheels again, the taxi had stopped shaking and my driver had regained control. The road was now clear of snow and there were no other cars to be seen up ahead.

It was the brakes, my driver gasped once we were past the wall of rock and had pulled into a dirt road running through the pine trees. She was struggling to catch her breath and I couldn't get a word out. Then she said it again. It was the brakes that saved us.

My winter could have been over in an instant, but now we were at a standstill. All the cars had gone by and we were alone among the trees. We had been saved by an invention, my driver said, and once she had got her breath back she explained that the car was equipped with a special braking system. Because it had not been her who was steering the car. It was the automatic emergency braking system which had ensured that it stayed on the road. She had braked when we went into a skid, but it was thanks to this emergency system that the brakes had not jammed and sent us straight into the truck's path. Or into the cars behind it. Or into the rock wall alongside us. Or across the road and down that steep slope. That was why the car had stayed on course. Because the braking system had taken control. I think it was the shock that led her to talk about the car's mechanics. That way she didn't have to talk about how terrified she had been.

Actually, she said, after she'd stepped out of the car and taken a walk around it, it was an accident on a forest road over the border in Sweden that had inspired a German engineer to invent the emergency braking system in our vehicle. He had skidded on an icy road and tried to brake. If there had been a truck ahead of him he would never have been able to invent his system. Instead, he had spun around and ended up in a ditch at the side of the road. She then launched into a detailed description of the technology behind this braking system and the various stages of development it had gone through during her time as a taxi driver, but I think she could tell that the technical details were not really getting through to me. Not that it didn't interest me, but all I could think of was that huge blue cab bearing down on us, the great wide face that we would have crashed into head-on had that engineer not come to our aid.

Not long afterward the taxi driver was ready to drive again. Once before she had been in a situation where the braking system had saved her from running off the road, but not with a truck coming toward her, she said, and with a tail of cars behind it. Now, though, we were heading for the guest house, only a couple of miles away. As it happened her cousin worked there. Susanne, her name was. They had both grown up in the area, just a little farther north. Susanne had also lived in France, in Toulouse. They had been there together. She was Jeanette, by the way. I told her my name was Tara. She didn't think that sounded French or Belgian. I explained that my mother was English. I didn't think her name sounded particularly Norwegian either, but I didn't say that.

We reached the guest house, having encountered hardly any more oncoming traffic and it was with relief that I got out of the car on a square in front of a red wooden building. My legs were still a little shaky and I noticed that my driver was also moving rather carefully when she got out and went in with me to say hello to her cousin.

I made sure that I was given a room that had not been used recently and I am now sitting at a little table, looking out on a pine forest where some of the trees have been blown down by the storm. I write on my paper, not in my green book. I have not written the address of the guest house in the book. I do not see myself coming back here. I wished for winter and I have winter. I have snow, I have more than a sprinkling, there is snow everywhere. There is snow on the paths behind the guest house and on the mountain that reaches up for miles and miles, but I am not going any farther, I may already have gone too far.

#470

I wish to turn toward spring. It is a difficult maneuver, though. Like bringing around a ship, I feel, a large vessel. My seasons machine has taken over, it has led me into more and more winter, it has been set to far too much snow, I try to stop, to brake, but it's not that easy.

Spring is usually something that comes all by itself. You feel a little cold, you long for it and suddenly there it is, a softness in the air, bright mornings. Now spring is something I have to build, but winter seems to have chilled me and so I sit here in a guest house in the snow. I can't move on, winter holds me fast in its hushed landscape.

In the middle of the night, around three o'clock, it starts to snow, sometimes a little earlier, sometimes later. There's a clock on the bedside table, an old clock radio, the radio is broken, but the clock works and the numbers are illuminated. I lost my phone ages ago and I've got used to living without clocks, but these days I wake to those luminous numerals and a soundless world. There's no wind and it strikes me that it must be the silence that wakes me, the absence of sound. It must be because it's snowing, but I don't get it, I mean how can the snow muffle the sounds when everything is already silent. It's as if the snow is antisound, as if it casts an additional layer of silence over everything, the sound level drops below zero and I lie in my bed, listening to less than nothing, even my own sounds are gone. Not for long, though, because then I draw breath and then I hear a very faint breeze, a rustling in the treetops, and I hear people in the corridor, little noises outside my room.

Every morning, after I've had breakfast, I park myself in the lobby. I tell the receptionist who has just come on duty that I arrived late the night before and probably haven't been registered yet. I sit there reading for a while then I get up and go outside. Into the open. Into the whiteness. Into far too much snow. I roam through the forest, along its paths, I walk uphill. I think of the paths through the forest near Clairon, in the flat country alongside the river, and of the autumn colors, but the paths here are sloping, they run uphill and downhill and every morning I climb up, then face about and walk back down, as if practicing turning around.

Today, amid all the white I came upon a church. I had lost my bearings, I think, and was close to going astray, but the church lay high up, I gazed down into the valley and in the distance I spotted a building that looked like my guest house.

Relieved at not being lost, I went for a walk around the church-yard. I tried the handle of the church door, but it was locked so I abandoned that idea and took a stroll among the gravestones instead. There were no footprints on the paths, I was the only person to have trodden the new-fallen snow. I glimpsed a few houses around about, but no people, or at any rate no one liv-ing, because I had suddenly come to think of all the bodies ly-ing under the gravestones. It gave me a strange sense of peace. A feeling of not being alone. There were people close by, lying in coffins or in urns. Our bodies were in different states, some were ashes, others were bones and some still had flesh on the bones, and skin, and clothes covering the skin, but we were all of the same stuff. They had names. I saw them on their stones. Many of the stones were beautifully carved, with polished sur-faces, some had decorative borders around the names or small snow-decked figures on top. Some monuments were smaller and simpler, while others were larger and more roughly hewn, somewhere between rock and gravestone. But there were names on all of them and dates on most, dates of birth and death.

The dates of death made me feel alone again. I had a date of birth. I had a name: Tara Selter, that was me. But no date of death. Not yet. My date of death could have been the eighteenth of November, I had already had one close shave and perhaps it would be the eighteenth of November, but I was alive, I had been saved by a special braking system, I had come to a halt. But I could have taken my driver to death with me. I could have taken the whole string of shocked motorists with me. We could all have been lying here. Simply because I wanted winter and snow. I had intruded on their eighteenth of November. I had to be careful, I told myself. I already know that I leave a mark.

I consume my world. I sustain burns and sprained ankles. But I also put other people in danger. I drag them out of their eighteenth of November. Out of their routine. I risk killing someone. I don't imagine that the world will repair itself, that if I lead people off course they will simply wake up again the next morning. I have to be careful. I am a danger to my surroundings, I tell myself, as I roam around in the snow. I drag people with me along snowy paths.

But not right here, in the snow, in the churchyard. I had wandered through fresh snow, I crossed no tracks, I was not in the way, I did no harm. Or hardly any. I did leave a trail of footprints but the snow would erase them when it started to fall during the night.

#472

I go to bed early every evening. I fall asleep quickly. I wake up in the middle of the night. If it hasn't already started snowing I lie in my bed and wait. The only sounds are very faint: a soft rustling in the treetops, the odd car in the distance and then, suddenly, all sound disappears. I tell myself that I know what is about to happen. It is the eighteenth of November returning, all sound disappears and then the snow starts to fall.

#473

Every day, in the early afternoon, long after I have returned from my wanderings, a truck turns into the forecourt of the guest house. It is blue, and I think it's the truck we almost collided with, Jeanette and I. I can't be sure, it belongs to a local trucking company and they have a number of rigs so it might not be the same one, but I think it is. The driver delivers goods to the kitchen, he leaves a pallet of cardboard boxes at the kitchen door and drives off again at a time which I believe would fit with when we met on the road. It must be him. I didn't see his face from our car, only the big blue cab bearing down on us.

I usually spend the afternoons in the lobby, reading or considering how to move on. I have ground to a halt. A sudden braking and now I can't get any further on my own. I need horsepower, a vehicle, to carry me out of winter, to help me turn around. I consider the blue truck, the tracks it leaves in the forecourt: tomorrow I may ask if I can hitch a ride.

#475

I had packed my things before installing myself in the lobby with my book and was sitting there reading when the truck driver walked in. I asked him if he was heading south and would be passing a railway station, and if so, could I hitch a ride? I was welcome to, he said. My idea had been for him to drop me off at the railway station in the nearest town, but he was going further south, he would be crossing the Bergen line, he said, and it would be easy for me to carry on from a station down there.

While he was unloading the goods for the kitchen I got my bag and paid my bill at the reception desk. I tucked the book I had been reading onto a shelf in the lobby where residents could help themselves to books left by previous guests. It was one of the couple I had taken from my parents' bookshelves. I took the other from my bag and put this and two more which I had long since finished on the shelf before climbing into the blue cab. Minutes later, after checking that the doors were locked, the driver turned the truck around in the forecourt swung out onto the road and headed south.

I felt safe in the truck. From the cab I could survey the countryside. I had a good view of the road and could watch the cars driving along beneath us: families, couples and lone motorists imprisoned in tiny vehicles. I'm not sure why I felt safe, I mean we could still have skidded off the road, we could have driven over the embankment, we could have tipped over, but we didn't.

From my vantage point up there next to the driver I could look out over the trees, which seemed very fragile now that so many of their fellows had been blown over, delicate plants that lay scattered on the ground, flung hither and thither by the storm. The driver told me about the storm, an autumn gale, he called it, but it must have been a spring gale which snapped those trees because I'm traveling toward spring and I have once more begun to gather together the pieces for my year. I think of March and I have written *March storm* in my green book. I have started looking for signs of spring and farther south, when we descended from the hills, there was already less snow.

I told the driver about my experience in the taxi. I didn't say that it must have been his truck which had almost crashed into us because neither he nor Jeanette would have any recollection of the incident, but he then proceeded to tell me even more about braking systems than I already knew. I said I felt safe in the truck, high above the road and that I really didn't like ordinary vehicles—sedans, family cars: small steel boxes with their false promises of safety.

After a few hours we stopped for a break and the driver insisted on sharing his packed lunch with me: rye bread with soused herring and cold rolled lamb with pickled beetroot. I told him that I already liked herring. And rye bread. And that I now also liked *lammerull med rødbete*. It was homemade, he said. All his wife's work. She always made sure he had plenty to eat when he was on the road. He might be away for days at a time, he might have to drive the length of Europe, not often, but when he did he had enough food for the whole trip. That way he felt he was still eating with his family.

When we came to the town where I was to catch the train he offered to drive me all the way to the station, but I refused the offer and got out of the truck at the turnoff. I didn't want to take him off his scheduled route, so I thanked him for the lift and walked into town along the shoulder as the truck disappeared into the distance.

The last train had already left, so I checked into the nearest hotel and have now resumed my seasonal journey. I have written the hotel's address in my seasons book, I have written about signs of spring and the train times to Bergen.

I have a sense of momentum. I'm sure spring is on its way, and with my scrambled eggs at the hotel I had chives, which are called *gressløk* in Norwegian and taste slightly of spring. But I don't want to rush the year. I won't go to the airport and cheat my way to spring air, it's in the waiting that spring becomes *spring* and so I wait at my hotel until it's time to go to the station, I wait for small signs of spring, for a thaw and warmer days.

#476

I took the morning train to Bergen only to find that I wasn't done with winter after all. Soon the countryside stretched out below us, white with patches of gray here and there: we had been steadily climbing through a landscape of rocks and snow. But by the time we reached the outskirts of Bergen, a couple of hours behind schedule, the landscape was no longer white and the snow had given way to rain.

In my compartment were two foreign students, apparently on their way to meet their future landlord. From the telephone conversation one of them was having I understood that they were planning to rent a room in the center of town, or two rooms as it turned out. They'd had an appointment with the owner of the property, but they wouldn't be able to make that now. The student who was on the phone obviously understood Norwegian and he was taking the details and translating for his companion. I could hear them arranging to view the room the following day instead. The owner would be there at 10 a.m., but if they got there earlier they would find the key on the ledge above the inside door. The room was unoccupied and could be reached by way of the fire escape. The outside door was usually open. To be on the safe side the one who spoke Norwegian spelled out the address for the other, who wrote it down. As did

I. I made a note of it in my seasons book, because it had occurred to me that if they weren't going to be moving in until the nineteenth I could use it till then.

At the station in Bergen there was a big map of the town. I quickly located my street on the map and on an unoccupied bench next to it I found an abandoned umbrella. I glanced around for a possible owner, but there was hardly anyone around so I took it with me. It was a flowery umbrella. I had never owned a flowery umbrella. A spring-flowered umbrella, I thought to myself as I stepped out into the rain.

It wasn't hard to find the address and before long I was standing at the foot of a gray steel fire escape. I went up the steps and sure enough: there at the top was an unlocked glass door leading to a corridor on which were five black doors, and on the ledge above the door of one of these—the first as you came in—was a key that fitted the lock in that door. It didn't take me long to get myself settled in the room, which was in fact two small rooms with a tiny kitchenette at the end of one of them. The only furniture was a couple of fold-up mattresses which were stacked in a corner, so I spread these out, switched on the heating, wrapped my coat around me and soon fell asleep.

During the night the rain turned to snow. It snowed for the rest of the night and this morning I woke to white roofs. I sat on the windowsill and gazed out at all the whiteness which I really longed to escape.

While I was sitting there the rain came on again and not long afterward I heard the first snow sliding off the roof. Moments later another clump slipped off with a soggy, rather grating sound that reverberated through the wall behind me. The movement of the snow made itself felt as a faint tremor at my back where I sat on the windowsill gazing out across the rooftops, from which clump after clump of wet snow was slithering and crashing into the streets.

Snow sliding off roofs is a spring sound and there is no doubt in my mind that spring is on its way, because even though it is autumn rain that is causing the night's snowfall to slither off the roof it is the sounds of spring that come to mind. I think of snow sliding off the roof and landing in old Selter's garden. That is the sound I hear and I remember a spring day in Clairon, although maybe it was still only February and not spring at all, or maybe it was March, but there had been several days of snow and frost and then, suddenly, it thawed. Thomas's father had been visiting us. It must have been just after we moved into the house because he hasn't been back since.

We were in the office, which had been Thomas's father's bedroom when he was a boy. He had shared it with his brother, Thomas's uncle, and their parents had slept in the room next door. We stood there, listening to the snow sliding off the roof while Thomas's father told us about winter in Clairon.

He had just said something about the snow in old Selter's garden, about how he and his brother had been playing in the piles of snow that had slid off the roof, even though his father—old Selter, as he called him—had forbidden them to play there because of the long icicles hanging from the gutter, sharp and ready to fall, when suddenly a huge icicle had snapped off and hit the ground right next to them.

Thomas laughed. Not at the story, which he had only half heard, but at his father calling his own father old Selter. Ah, but now he was old Selter, Thomas said. I smiled briefly, but that I clearly should not have done Thomas's father was furious, he turned away and stayed mad for the rest of the day. He didn't like the idea. He didn't like the thought of time passing. He didn't like the thought of aging. He didn't like the thought of Thomas being young Selter. He had gone to the market that morning with Thomas and he hadn't liked that. Walking alongside his grown-up son. Because that meant he was old and he didn't want to be old.

Now as the snow slides off the roof what I hear is the sound of spring and I think of spring and summer and autumn and I don't mind that time is passing.

#479

I sailed from Bergen this morning before the snow started sliding off the roof and now I'm on my way across the North Sea. I've noted the departure times of the ferries in my seasons book and I feel it again: the passage of the seasons. I hear it when I'm up on deck, the drone of the engines, a rope slapping against the ship's side again and again.

The lights of the harbor disappeared behind us as we sailed off in the gray morning light. It was quite windy. There's still a bit of a breeze, but not much, there's no storm in sight, I'm expecting a smooth crossing. I've checked the meteorologist's curves and forecasts. I'm expecting spring and I'm dressed for spring. It's cold when I go up on deck in my light jacket. I found it in a secondhand shop in Bergen, pale gray with a touch of green to it. It may not go so well with my flowery umbrella, but it made me think of spring so I left my winter coat behind in the secondhand shop. I've bought a pair of ankle boots, I'm traveling light and springlike. A little optimistic, perhaps, but I'm heading for places with mild weather, gentle breezes, a touch of green.

#482

I arrived at dusk. It was a while before we were able to disembark, then I had to go through passport control and immigration and then, when I eventually made it to my train, it had trouble starting so it was well into the night before it finally set off into the darkness. I tried to think of it as gentle spring darkness, but it was late and I fell asleep on the train.

We arrived in London early in the morning and I went straight out to look for a hotel with a vacant room. There was no snow in the streets, no rain. It was neither cold nor warm. There was light and noise in the dark city. There were open shops and people in the streets. I tried to think of spring, but no one was dressed as if spring were just around the corner. I told myself that daylight might bring some sign of spring and it didn't take me long to find a hotel with a vacant room that I could gain access to straight away.

It wasn't until the next day that I found spring. Or actually, the next day I found everything. I went into several shops, looking for signs of spring, at first cheerfully and inquisitively, then bewildered, overwhelmed and eventually almost stunned by the seasonal havoc that met my eyes. I'm not sure what confused me most: the shelves piled high with fruit, berries and vegetables from every time of the year and part of the world or the variety of the packaging. I wove my way around shelves and cabinets, crates and mounds of produce. I saw containers of all shapes and forms: hexagonal ones, square ones, small rectangles and large ovals, medium-sized cups with clear domed plastic lids and square tubs with sharp corners. There were flat trays in plastic and paper, odd-shaped baskets and crackling bags perforated to let air in or out. There were long containers with stalks of rhubarb and little pots of herbs that carried on growing on the shelf in the bright spring light. There were rows and rows of packaged fruit, bags and trays with all sorts of odd closing mechanisms, with zippers and buttons and little rubber bands. I passed little baskets of blueberries, raspberries and strawberries nestling on soft pads. I saw yellow string bags full of lemons, orange ones full of oranges, green ones full of limes and a single burgundy bag of red grapes. There were whole shelves of sliced fruit, clear plastic trays full of all sorts of fruit in every shape imaginable: diced or in batons, sliced or in triangles or scooped into yellow or green balls. There were vegetables in bags and cartons, julienned or grated or chopped or sliced in rings. There were tubs of mixed salads, complete with dressing, garnish, forks and spoons, all neatly packed in bags, and I wandered around completely unable to choose. I had forgotten what went with spring.

I thought of spring in old Selter's garden. The early spring flowers, the tiny chive spears poking through the earth and parsley from the autumn coming to life and preparing to grow for a while before abruptly bolting. The Swiss chard that had languished in the winter darkness and was now starting to sprout again from dark-green hearts; the last leeks, a little floppy after a winter in the garden, that had to be taken in before it was too late; the onions in the shed; the potatoes, if there were any left, and soon the first rhubarb unfurling, the spinach shoots appearing, the surviving artichokes, their pointed leaves springing from the winter-worn plants while the grayish-brown remains from last year disintegrated on the ground around them, and later still the green asparagus: first the very smallest shoots which had self-seeded and, a few weeks later, the tall pale-green spears, more and more of them, until midsummer, when they would be left to go on growing into tall, dark-green bushes.

I thought of the market in Clairon. Shoppers in baggy spring coats, housewives and elderly gentlemen holding their baskets open for the loose fruit and vegetables to be placed into them in rough layers, topped off with a brown paper bag of grapes; young men and women with printed shopping bags, passersby with rustling plastic bags.

I put nothing in my basket. I dragged it behind me, swaying about on its wonky wheels, unable to decide. I went from shop to shop like a creature bewildered by the bright light, torn between my quest for spring and the colors of all four seasons.

In the end it was the words that came to my rescue and I made for the checkout with my basket of spring names: *spring greens*, *spring onions* and a plastic tub of *spring soup*. I left the shop clutching a little bagful of spring, not much, but enough for me to feel that I was on the right track.

Back in my room I ate my spring soup, cold and indefinable of flavor, then I put my vegetables in my bag and asked at reception for directions on how to find my way south, toward spring.

#497

I am out of winter. The air here is mild. *Spring air*, I think to myself as I bike along wet roads, in fine rain. Spring rain, I don't bike far, I take one day at a time. I've got used to the roads, the traffic. I've got used to the houses where I rent a room for a day or two. I've got used to kitchens and stoves and fridges. I chop spring greens briskly with a good sharp knife from the drawer. I have found radishes and spinach, I have found sunny days with no snow, with soft breezes, and yesterday I found a chair in a garden shed, so now I can sit in the sunshine—not for long and I wear my spring jacket, but there is more sunshine to come if I travel farther south.

I bike from one small town to another, along narrow roads, past green fields. Well, a few are still brown, but in many the fresh, new shoots are up. I feel the soft, damp air on my skin. Enough, surely, to call this spring.

At the first house I stayed in I found a bike in the toolshed. I hovered around it for a couple of days then took it out of the shed, greased the chain with oil I found on a shelf, bought saddlebags and elastic cords to secure my bag to the luggage rack. I went for short rides around the neighborhood, then I came across a rain poncho and a pair of rubber boots that were a bit too big for me and left my warm woolens in the poncho's place.

Biking warms you up, you get used to the rain and the warmth. I bike along in a gentle breeze and watery sunlight. If there is a light shower of rain I slip on the poncho, if the rain intensifies I take shelter for a while, and so I progress: slowly and cautiously through springtime.

I still have my flowery umbrella. It is rolled up in my bag, and now I also have covers for my saddlebags because I am fond of biking through the spring rain, I am fond of the shifting skies, with bursts of sunlight giving way to cloud, I am fond of gravel paths and of afternoons spent riding against the wind.

I note the names of towns and roads in my seasons book. I ride along bike paths and over small bridges that carry me across rivers and canals. I look for signs of spring and I cook spring dishes in strange kitchens. There are empty houses to be found on the eighteenth of November. I write the addresses of the empty houses and the spring dishes in my book. I find shops along the way where I can stock up on supplies and I write that it is spring and that the fields are green. I write of patch kits and chains that suddenly come off, of bike shops with air pumps outside which you can use when the shop's closed.

#504

The tempo has speeded up, the days fly by. I write *April* in my seasons book. I am traveling south and thinking of holidays in spring weather, I think of Easter holidays in England, I think of Lisa and her summer weather. I think of Thomas and then I pedal harder, I feel the sweat on my back under the rain poncho and my feet in the too-big rubber boots. And so I make headway, so things move a little faster, I have to concentrate on the hills, I zoom down, I battle my way up and that stops me from thinking.

I survey the landscape and write names in my seasons book. Place after place. Name after name. I write about the wind in my hair, the rain on my face, my cold hands on the handlebars.

#508

On the first Sunday after the first full moon after the spring equinox. That's when Easter falls. But I have no Sundays, I have no full moons or equinoxes. So how can I have Easter? And who comes up with things like that anyway? Who comes up with holidays that follow the movements of suns and moons and planets? My year cannot be governed by the heavens, because the heavens are always the same, I have to find my spring in the fields and on the paths, I have to find my Easter in the shops. I seek Easter weather, but Easter weather can be anything. I remember hail in April, I remember Easter sunshine and Easter showers in our garden in Brussels. I remember Easter in England, I remember warm days and light frosts.

I find Easter in my memory. I remember Easter eggs. Lisa and I on a rug. It must have been a family party at my mother's brother's house, for a birthday maybe, or a wedding anniversary, possibly my grandparents'—all I remember is the eggs. Lisa and I had asked if we could borrow some of my cousin's toys, but that wasn't possible, so my mother produced a couple of our books from her bag and we were sitting on the rug reading them when our aunt came over to us with a little basket. In the basket were four beautiful eggs, possibly wooden and quite heavy. I remember the weight of the eggs in my hand and their colors, they were painted, I think, yellow, pale-gray and green, delicately patterned.

This is for you, my aunt said, smiling at us. She handed them to me because I was the oldest, but they were meant for both of us because she looked at Lisa, whose face lit up at the sight of the beautiful eggs, and then at me as I took the basket from her, delighted by this lovely present. Just then another party guest came over to say hello to our aunt and she disappeared into the throng in the living room.

A moment later, while Lisa was taking the eggs out of the basket, I jumped up because a thought had just struck me: I had forgotten the cardinal rule. I dashed over to my aunt, who was standing talking to a man I didn't know and said in a breathless rush: *Thank you, Auntie Kate, thank you so much*. She gave me a puzzled look so I thanked her again for the lovely eggs she had given us, the eggs in the little basket. She looked at me for a moment then she hooted with laughter.

Oh, I wasn't giving them to you to keep, she said, her eyes meeting those of her companion, who was now laughing along with her. The eggs weren't a present. What made me think that? They were only for us to play with, she told me as I backed away. Maybe it was disappointment at learning that the beautiful eggs were not ours to keep, maybe it was mortification at having misunderstood, or maybe, more than anything, it was their shared laughter that made me feel so embarrassed, but whatever it was the pleasure was gone and just then I saw my aunt exchange another glance with the unknown man, a long-suffering sort of look, a little wiggle of her eyebrows, something she tended to do if we made a mistake, if one of us mixed up French and English, or if we forgot to say *please* and *thank you* when we were visiting her.

Lisa was still sitting on the floor with an egg in each hand, but I had lost interest. I told her the eggs weren't ours, but she still thought they were beautiful. I felt it took far too long for her to lose interest as well, but eventually she did tire of playing with them. We set the basket down very carefully on a windowsill and went out into the garden to find our cousin.

Later, back on the train, I told my parents about the little basket of painted eggs and my mother tried to explain my aunt's response. Perhaps we had misheard her. Perhaps what she'd said was: *This is for you to play with*. But I knew that wasn't what she had said. Perhaps, our mother said, she had been given the little basket of eggs herself by the very guest she'd been standing next to. Perhaps she had been trying to salvage the situation, not wanting him to think that she'd given his present away. Perhaps, perhaps, my father said and we didn't speak of it again.

When we changed trains in London my father vanished into the crowd and reappeared minutes later with two large chocolate eggs in shiny yellow paper. I remember how carefully I bore my Easter egg when we resumed our journey. It was almost too big for my hands and difficult to hold. Lisa was too little to carry hers, but I carried mine gently onto the train and sat with it in front of me on the little table, and when we reached our destination I carried it off the train again without it breaking. I can no longer remember when I ate my egg. I don't remember how it tasted, nor do I remember the sound of the yellow foil when I unwrapped it. They must have been there, the taste and the sounds, but all I remember is that train journey with a big yellow egg sitting in front of me.

#512

The Easter I found in memory did not take me any further in my search for spring. Nor did it bring me any closer to spring to find hot cross buns in a supermarket or a shop selling Easter table napkins and little chocolate bunnies in a yellow plastic string bag. As I biked on with my booty in my saddlebags it occurred to me that it seemed a bit desperate. That these things had nothing to do with Easter or spring. They were just props. Something to put in my green book along with Easter addresses, signs of spring, temperatures and hours of sunshine.

#513

And yet. All at once I have the wind at my back. I bowl along gravel bike paths, across bridges and beside canals, the sun comes out, my seasons machine is working and it doesn't matter if it's a November day. It doesn't matter if my spring is built out of weird props. I'm being blown forward in my year. I pedal along with my spring lies, little green lies, or yellow. My November day lets go, it loses its grip, I have ridden away from it. I have beaten the unmoving, Easterless November sky, last night the sky was overcast, but today the spring sun is shining and I am riding south.

#519

And then, all at once, there they are: newborn lambs in a field in Cornwall. I think of the meteorologist—she was right. There *are* Easter lambs here. I ride on and there's not just one field of them, but several. Ewes with tiny little lambs. I stop, amazed. It isn't cold here, in fact it's quite warm. Spring has come. I turn off the path and cycle along the edge of the field, and then I see a sign saying *Spring Farm* and *Bed & Breakfast*. I think of ultra-spring, essence of spring, concentrated spring, and I check in.

#526

It's not easy to hold on to spring. It slips between my fingers as soon as I stop moving. I sit by the window in my cabin behind my spring farm and from here I can see ewes with lambs in the field. There are sheds full of spring, the sheep lamb, the cows calve, the pastures are green, there are meadows and fields sown with winter seed.

But something is missing. I don't write this in my book, but I am writing it here. Something in the air or somewhere inside me. Sensations and smells, or possibly sounds. The morning explosion of birdsong, the scent of growing things. The air seems too thin, maybe it's something from the newly sprung trees that is lacking, a greenness in the atmosphere, vernal chemistry, pollen dust, I don't know, but even if the fields are green it's hard to summon up a sense of spring.

I don't write this in my book, that there is no spring in the air, that there are no sounds from above. It's not something you can see, but I can smell the emptiness. I can hear it. There is no singing.

In the morning I knock on the farmhouse door and check in to the cabin. I act as though I have just arrived and leave my bike in the yard. Not long afterward a young family arrives. They have come to see the November spring lambs and all the little calves. We are shown around the farm by the owner and he explains how they do things. It's more practical to let the sheep and the cows have their babies in the autumn, he says. He actually says *babies*. For the benefit of the three school-age children, I suppose. To the rest of us he talks about block calving, autumn lambing and the advantages of systematized breeding. It's a matter of time and labor management. When the berry and fruit harvesting is over, and the autumn sowing, there are still plenty of seasonal workers around. Which means extra hands to help with the sheep and the cattle, the weather is mild enough for them to lamb and calve during the autumn months, they then have time to grow over the winter and they're ready for the spring.

Behind the farmhouse are a number of sheds containing more ewes and lambs that think it is spring. There are horses for rent, so I rent a horse, a placid creature, and we go for a ride through the woods, a nice quiet ride, but these are autumn woods. I can't keep spring up.

#543

I left the bike in a garden shed in Plymouth. I deposited the saddle bags and my rubber boots in a corner of the shed, but I still have the poncho. I boarded a ferry and now I'm on a train, bound for summer. I sense a change. The plants help me along. I think of asparagus. Of rhubarb and early strawberries. I'm ready for summer and I'm on my way. Longing for sunshine. Full of anticipation. I don't need scorching days, just a pleasant summer with some sun and the sounds of the shore.

I think of my sister. I have considered dragging her through summer with me, going to see her and telling her the whole story: pack a bag and let's go.

And then I think of Thomas. I think of his gaze. The feeling of warm skin and summer days. It occurs to me that I could go to Clairon, that I could go and get him, that he might come traveling with me after all, that we could travel into summer together.

I think of his footsteps on the stairs on a summer afternoon. The wood creaking at every step he takes. He is back from the post office. I hear him go upstairs to tidy up in the office, he puts some books away. I go upstairs, we have work to do, but before too long we end up next door in bed anyway.

I know, though. That he won't come away with me. That I can't use summer as an inducement. He'll tell me that I'll have to find summer on my own. I won't go and get anyone, not even my sister. I'll get there on my own. How could I ask them to come with me? How could I drag them into my eighteenth of November?

#562

I have found summer. Summer in November. Or early summer anyway. On a beach near Montpellier. The weather here is summer-warm, with sun in the middle of the day. I note temperatures and hours of sunshine in my seasons book and I write that there aren't many tourists because it's early in the season. This means, though, that it's not hard to find a vacant summer cottage and there's no problem in getting a table in a summer café.

I'm staying in an empty house by the water, in the morning I eat strawberries in my kitchen with a view of the beach. I buy asparagus and fresh fish and soon I will be moving on, bound for warmer days. I no longer need my rain poncho so I have folded it up and put it in a cupboard under the stairs along with the umbrella and when I go up the stairs to my bedroom overlooking the water I catch a very faint sound from the treads under my feet, a nascent summer creak.

I have found blankets and summer cushions. I took them out onto the terrace and on a couple of nights I have slept out there. They are spotted with mildew and it was cold when I woke, it is damp in the mornings, but still the stairs creaked when I carried my cushions and blankets back up to the bedroom, not much, it is not quite the creak of summer, but the sun streams through the window and soon I will travel on down the coast, because now I am ready for heat. For sun, for sand, for summer nights.

#578

It's not hard to find summer in November. You follow the stream of people wishing for summer and the farther south you go the more people there are on the beach, on the promenades. More people and fewer clothes.

I think more about the bodies now that it is summer. I think more about skin, about hands and feet and arms and legs, now that I can see them on the street. The bodies on the beach lead me to thoughts of Thomas. I bring him into the picture. I remember that bodies can be naked and Thomas appears, because the clothes are gone. As far as I'm concerned beachgoers can keep all their arms and legs, but if I go on thinking, Thomas takes over.

I can't act as if he doesn't exist. As if he isn't sitting in a house somewhere while I lie in the sunshine and watch the bathers. I can't sit in a bar and speak to one of the beachgoers and invite him back to my house and sit with him on my balcony and drink wine and then take him to my bed. That is not possible because I know that sooner or later he will turn into Thomas before my eyes.

#584

I kept an eye on the house. I walked by it in the morning and in the middle of the day. I walked by it in the evening. My house.

My summer house. It is set back a little on one of the streets running down to the beach. There was no one to be seen so I went back the next day. I couldn't find a key, I looked under planters and in a shed at the back of the garden and in the end I broke in, it wasn't hard to do, I found a basement window at the back of the house, the side facing the garden and a terrace with a table and a couple of chairs on it, all ready in the summer weather.

I think it's been a long time since anyone lived in this house, but now I am living here. The garden furniture was sitting there as if it had been waiting for me. It wasn't difficult to pry the window open and slip into the basement.

The house was habitable but dusty. On the table in the kitchen lay a bunch of keys and when I went upstairs I knew that this house could be my home until the end of the summer. It was the sound of the stairs. I felt at home and in my seasons book I wrote that it is summer. I have written the addresses of Spanish hotels, I have written about railway stations and buses, I have written the names of small towns and streets and now I have written about my house. That it is yellow. That the market in the square is open in the mornings and that I only need to step out of my front door and turn toward the town and I am five minutes away from the exuberance of summer.

#592

For the first time it occurs to me: that Thomas is right when he says I have to find a way out on my own. With your sense for detail, he said. I don't know if there is any way out to be found, but I observe the details, the parts of the bodies, human details. A big toe with some dark hairs sprouting from it, a foot in a sandal. I look down at the floor under the next table in the café. I notice the nape of a neck in front of me in the train going to a neighboring town. A hand, or two hands actually, working together, tying up one of the boats in the harbor. The hands turn in an intricate dance and the boat is tied up. I stand looking out to sea, I consider asking whether I can sail with it when it leaves, but can one sail through the eighteenth of November? I don't know, but I do know that I have summer. Perhaps I shouldn't ask for more.

I walk into the town and sit down in a café. My sense for detail draws my eye to a man with a newspaper in front of him. He keeps putting his finger to the bridge of his glasses, nudging them back into place. Then he looks up. My sense for detail sees him smile, but then it is gone again, that sense, and I take my book out of my bag.

I put my hair up and find a sleeveless summer dress. My hair has grown long and in the morning I go into town to have it cut. I feel lighter once I have seen my hair fall onto the floor under the chair. That is something I have lost, I tell myself, my hair and my hope. That is hair that Thomas has touched. It falls to the floor and is swept up. Now I have only eighteenth of November hair on my head.

#605

In the evening I go out on the town. Not only on one single evening but first one, then another, and a couple of days later

I go back again. I dance, I don't talk much because the music is loud. We speak different languages, but in simple sentences that are almost drowned out by the music.

I ruffle my hair and say: *I have lost my hair and my hope*. We speak English. *My hair and my hope*, I say and carry on dancing. The next night I say it in German, and in French, but then there is no more to be had from that remark. *Meine Haare und meine Hoffnung. Mes cheveux et mes espoirs.*

I dance, I whirl and twirl, and I think of my days in Clairon. I have a mood again, I think to myself. I think *joyful* and *without hope*. I drink cocktails with ice cubes in them, I dance, I toast with evening revelers while nibbling large olives and Basque guindilla peppers. I dance with women, but mostly with men. The room is full of detail and I notice all of it.

All the signals. I register a range of all but forgotten signals coming into play. From my arms and my legs. My fingers, which cannot resist twirling what's left of my hair. I adjust my dress, we read each other, draw closer, then draw back. I drink sour cocktails with a man who casts sidelong glances at my hand and not until later do I realize that he is looking for signs of a ring. There is a slightly paler band on his finger and I ask him if he has his ring in his pocket. He does. He shows it to me and I tell him that Thomas and I have never had rings. We didn't feel that signals were necessary. A superfluous detail, I say. It is him who informs me that what we are nibbling are Basque guindilla peppers. He has lived in Navarra and he tries to teach me to say it in Basque: that I have lost my hair and my hope, but it's too difficult, I stumble over the details of the words, so instead we talk about pre-Indo-European languages, but not until later, when we are strolling in the dark. Our conversation goes around in circles. I have told him about the eighteenth of November, but I can tell that he doesn't believe me.

Late in the evening I walk back to my house. I am wearing shoes that go *click* and *clack* in the darkness, *click*, *click*, *clack* they say. I falter but I do not stop. I know that if I bring an evening reveler back to my house it is Thomas's details that I will call up. I send my signals to bed and sit down in the darkness behind the house.

My eye for detail turns inward, to the image of Thomas, then outward again. To the night sky, because I have caught sight of the sky at night. I have no telescope, but the night is dark. I recognize a number of my friends from the lawn in Clairon. I hear the sounds, a couple of nocturnal joggers running past my fence at a steady pace, although I cannot see them because the bushes around the terrace hide the road from my view. A child wails and a woman with an old voice tries to soothe it. A man and a woman walk past deep in conversation. Then a group goes by and later two women who suddenly burst out laughing.

I hear all the summer languages, they mingle with one another, I hear Spanish and English and German and then I hear Finnish and, a little later, an Asian language, then a Scandinavian one. Norwegian, I think.

#631

I don't go out at night any more. I stick to the sky and the passersby. I stick to the sounds of summer, to the languages, to the stars at night. I have visited the local observatory and seen parts of a gigantic pale gray moon, far too large.

I listen to the voices. To the words and the music. During the day I stroll around the town, I go into shops and wander up and down a pebble beach near my house. I collect different colored pieces of sea glass and put them in a clear jar on my windowsill. I have been here so long now that I know a lot of the town's summer visitors, the assistants in the shops and the waiters in the cafés and even though they don't recognize me this makes me feel at home. I hold on to summer and listen to summer languages. I pick up words that sound like summer, I write them in my book and if I hear someone say *Weihnachtsgeschenke* I quickly leave. I think: the heart of summer, consummate summer, concentrated summer and on my way back to my house I try to say *Wahljahreszeit*, but the word ties my tongue in knots even though I do my best to follow the rhythm as I walk along.

#639

I am preparing for the end of my summer. I am thinking of autumn. I am thinking of the house in Clairon, of autumn rain, but it is not something I miss. I don't miss the sounds of the house, the rain on the roof, the water in the pipes. I don't dream of going back. To the creak of the door handle. To letters and packages landing on the hall floor. To cup on saucer. To smoke coiling up from the chimney. To bird in tree, hand on wall, silhouettes in rain down by the fence.

I miss Thomas's footsteps on the stairs, but it is footsteps on summer stairs I miss. Not November stairs. I don't miss

Thomas in the eighteenth of November, I don't miss the house in Clairon.

I have stairs in my house, I have a creak when I go down or up, but that is all I have. When I lie in my bed with my window open to the night there is silence in the house. Nothing creaks and no one goes up or down the stairs.

#649

I am drifting toward late summer. Very slowly. Toward the north. There was a faint melancholy in the metallic click as I turned the key in the front door, but now I am on my way. I left the key behind a small pile of bricks in the garden shed because I will be back. That is what I am thinking. I will come back, because I have constructed summer and summer will come again. I pack away my colorful summer lies and now I am locking doors and moving toward late summer and toward autumn. Toward November, toward true November days, but that time has not yet come and I don't write it in my seasons book, because I want late summer and cool evenings.

I am making for late summer cities and I am thinking of autumn streets. I have written *Madrid* in my seasons book, I have traveled farther northward, I have studied the meteorologist's tables and found late-summer houses on the computer at my hotel, and now I feel the change, a stirring, an attentive tristesse. Summer is over, I walk with my jacket over my arm, my spring jacket is now an autumn jacket. I don't need it today, but when a cloud passes over the sun I'll be ready.

#654

There is a tremulousness, a quiet form of panic. I am looking for September. I am looking for places that feel like September in Clairon, a misty morning, a nip in the air, days that have wrested themselves free of summer warmth. There are more clothes on the streets, less skin. There are jackets and shoes here. I retreat indoors, I sense a certain restlessness, but nothing happens. Yesterday evening I went to the theater, but all I could see were people trapped within a space, on a stage. They roam restlessly around but can find no way out.

#655

It is quiet here. It is morning and I am sitting on a bench by a canal but there is no movement. I gaze at the water, which is brown and still. Or rather, there is scarcely any movement. The water flows so slowly that you have to fix your eye on a leaf that has landed on the surface if you want to see the movement occur, and then the leaf moves, a very slight movement.

My machine has stopped running. I think *September* and there is a leaf on the water and everything is about to grind to a complete halt.

In my seasons book I have written about mild August and early September. I have written *Arcachon* and *Bordeaux* and *La Rochelle*. I have followed the Atlantic coast and gone north. I have written down train times and hotels, all the things that I usually write down and yet it feels as though my year has ground to a complete halt.

#658

I am not a traveler. I move every now and again, but that is not travelling. I simply move a little farther north. I try to capture the taste of September. I buy apples and pears. I buy grapes and berries. I order autumn dishes and draw my jacket closer around my body.

I read of winter and spring and summer in my seasons book. I write *September* and think of white winter lies and all the many colors, green spring onions and the deep midnight blue of summer lies, golden morning lies in August, all the browns and reds and grays, but my lies are growing thinner and thinner now, they are pale gray and white and pastel-colored, but they are growing more and more transparent with every day. I can always sense November, but I write *September*. In a museum I study some Roman glasses, colored, milky. That is how it is. My lies have become a thin layer of glass. You can see through them, they have a hint of color to them, a thin layer of past times, of wear, only a touch of pigment, but I can see it: these glasses are full of November.

#667

And then, all at once, I found September. Unexpected September. Outside the statistical pattern, because I suddenly remembered my excessively mild days in Cologne. I was bound for winter and the air on the square outside the station had been far too warm, but now I can feel September, because the streets are delivering September air.

I got off the train and walked out onto the cathedral square, where the cathedral reared up to one side of me. The last time I was here I was wishing for December and January and the temperature had knocked me off course, but now all I feel is a lightness in the air. Sixty-three degrees and a gentle breeze.

On the square I was met by a soft wind. I went into the church, I gazed at the colors of the stained-glass windows in the dim light, then the sun broke through for a moment and the whole cathedral was lit up by a brilliant burst of kaleidoscopic light. Every corner was flooded with color, high and low, playing on the ceiling and on the wall and in the shadows on the floor, before fading once more. A tranquil light. September in color.

#671

My unease is gone and I have adjusted to this September day. I have found a hotel and I stroll around the city. Summer has closed down. Autumn has arrived, a soft sigh, a gentle day.

I feel at home when I sit down on a bench and consider the yellow leaves. I feel at home in the streets and in the cafés. It isn't hard to get the days to pass. I keep myself entertained, I see films and plays and go to concerts. A quiet curiosity attracts me to museums and exhibitions. I write it all down: a street on which the wind suddenly picked up, an exhibition by which I am caught and held for hours and which draws me back again the following day, a snug corner in a café where I read a book. All of this speaks of autumn, a light and curious autumn. A circle being closed. I am stretching myself. I have reached September and will carry on into October and when I reach November I can start all over again: a year, a template, an open seasons machine that I can climb aboard again and again.

#682

I had feared it, but I had never really thought it would happen. I don't know why. I mean, why wasn't I prepared? I should have guessed. That it might happen. A theft. A banal bag theft. But my bag is not just a bag. My bag is everything. All I own. If it is gone I am gone. Almost. But it has come back. Everything has come back. Almost. Everything I need has come back. But the fright has stayed with me. It has not gone, even though I have my bag back. So now I have both the fright and the bag and I carry both of them with me. But I no longer have my seasons book.

I had arrived in Düsseldorf to the same mild afternoon weather that I know from Cologne. There is a ridge of high pressure somewhere to the east of the city. I have called it September, but I had gone in search of October. In search of clear skies and somewhat cooler air and when I checked the meteorologist's databases on the computer at my hotel in Cologne I saw that I would find clear skies in Düsseldorf.

So the day before yesterday I arrived in Düsseldorf. Already at the station in Cologne I had noticed that there seemed to be a lot more passengers than on the other times I had been there. It was around two in the afternoon and I got on the first train to Düsseldorf, but only after I was settled in my seat did I realize that I was on a local train which stopped at every station, picking up passengers. And not just passengers but soccer fans on their way to Düsseldorf. Not that they were rude or rowdy; on the contrary, they were polite and affable. A bit tipsy and toasting. It was all very loud, jolly and a little disconcerting for anyone who was not a soccer fan but merely a September traveler bound for October.

I was offered a can of beer, which I accepted, albeit a little uncertainly. I thought: *September beer* and *September game*, but I think that was to avoid being knocked off course. I don't often encounter such festivity on a train and my previous journeys to and from Cologne must have been later in the afternoon because I couldn't remember any soccer fans or revelry or beer on other eighteenths of November.

My fellow passengers were on their way to a match between the Düsseldorf home team and what must have been a team from Cologne and there were fans from both sides on the train. There was an air of pregame fever, but it was all very good-natured, even though they belonged to different teams and wore different colored scarves: red and white for the one team, black and red for the other.

It was apparently an important match. A question of promotion or relegation but which for whom no one yet knew. In a couple of hours the matter would be settled and some of these passengers would be on the winning side, some on the losing side. Some would be moving up to another series or division or whatever it's called, others would move down. Or some would stay up and others would stay down. I wasn't altogether sure what the result of this seemingly crucial game would mean because I had not been aware that it was being played on the eighteenth of November.

The train was packed, people were swaying in the aisles, some were sitting on the floor by the door and the floor itself was dotted with little puddles of beer, puddles of fellowship, as if beer was what bound the two factions to one another—bound us to one another. So I raised my can of beer, first to the one side then to the other and drained it as the train became busier and busier and I began to wonder whether I ought to give my seat to one of my more unsteady fellow passengers, but then we were in Düsseldorf and at the station we poured out of the train and were washed along the platform and down the stairs. A phalanx of police officers was waiting in the entrance hall and only then did I begin to find the situation slightly unpleasant. It wasn't quite clear whether the police were expecting fighting or fun and games and I hurried off into the city center as the crowds of soccer fans spread out into the streets or started looking for transportation to the stadium where the game was to be played.

It was a sunny afternoon in Düsseldorf. Slightly cooler than in Cologne perhaps and not as cloudy. As I walked through the city in my search for October and a vacant hotel room I felt a faint frisson of delight at the vagueness of the situation: that there was something I didn't know about the eighteenth of November, that there might be small surprises hidden in there, that there was still some excitement left. I felt a sudden rush of pleasure at this lack of knowledge, not because I thought I knew everything about the eighteenth of November, but I did know a lot and there was also a lot that I could learn if I so wished, but at this particular moment there was no way I could discover anything about the result of the match. I had no clue. I was a novice in soccer's eighteenth of November.

I briefly considered joining the fun. I could go to a soccer game for the first time in my life, I told myself, but I quickly dismissed this thought because finding a hotel where I could spend the night proved to be no easy matter. I inquired at a number of hotels near the station, but only the fifth, a small hotel ten minutes' walk from the station where few soccer fans were likely to be staying, had any vacancies.

That evening I followed the game on the television in a bar near the hotel. The home team won and would seemingly now move up to the next division, but this victory was achieved only in overtime, during which tension mounted in the bar, although by this time I was losing interest. All of those watching the game on the big screen seemed to be fans of the home team and when the final whistle blew the bar erupted, but after drinking so many toasts the beer was making me sleepy and I quietly slipped out and went back to the hotel.

Yesterday I woke up with a bit of a hangover. I went back to sleep and woke up again just after midday. I went out and picked up a not particularly October-like sandwich somewhere nearby and in the midafternoon, once the sun had broken through, I went for a walk around the city. As I walked I could sense the time for the game approaching, I could almost feel the city falling quiet around me, the traffic thinned out and a large proportion of the city's inhabitants must either have gone to the game or moved indoors. I saw televisions on in some of the cafés and pizzerias I passed, with a few fans wearing scarves or T-shirts in the home team's colors parked in front of them, apart from that there was no way of telling who supported which team. I presume that most of the color-sporting fans had gone to the stadium to watch the game in person.

I wandered around the city, went down a flight of stone steps leading to the Rhine and carried on alongside the river. There weren't many people around. The occasional person or couple perched here and there on the stone wall on the quayside, a jazz band was playing on one of the floating restaurants and I sat myself down in a black plastic chair in the sunshine and had a beer while a few late lunchers enjoyed a meal at a nearby table.

I found myself thinking that I had acquired a taste for beer and then I found myself thinking of Oktoberfest. Whether Oktoberfest would be my next festival. Whether it would be my final stop before November came around again, and I wondered whether I might be able to find a party to go to. An Oktoberfest for people who had never met before, because I wasn't sure that I would automatically be included in the party as had happened on the train with the soccer fans.

After a little while I continued my walk along the riverside promenade, taking in the ships, the bridges and the long gray-stone quayside. I'm not sure whether it was because I wasn't paying attention, or because I had been sitting drinking beer in the sunshine or whether it was simply a combination of random factors, but suddenly a man came biking past me, I heard the rattle of an old bike with a rusty chain or a wheel that kept knocking against one of the mudguards. Maybe it was the sound that distracted me because before I knew it he had grabbed my bag, which was over my shoulder, wrested it out of my hands, quite roughly, I felt, and as I staggered back he managed to slip it off my arm, so deftly and so quickly that I had no time to react. All I saw was that he was wearing the home team colors, both scarf and hat, the latter pulled well down over his ears. Other than that he was wearing a dark-blue hoodie and a pair of dark sweatpants with a narrow white stripe down the side which was clearly visible when—still with my bag in his hand—he swung around in front of me and disappeared up a ramp leading from the promenade into the city center.

I shouted after him and set off in pursuit, but he was long gone before I reached the ramp. Up on the street I looked around for him as I struggled to catch my breath, but he must have cut across the sparse traffic at a red light and disappeared down one of the narrow streets on the other side of the road.

I was in shock, I was in despair and I felt naked without my bag. It had crossed my mind that such a thing could happen, but I had considered it unlikely. For one thing, my bag was pretty worn and shabby and didn't look likely to contain anything of value, and for another I definitely did not look like the kind of person who would be likely to carry anything of value. For safety's sake I always carry an extra credit card in my jacket pocket, but I had not thought it necessary to take any greater precaution than that of frequently dividing up my cash and keeping it in several different places on my person. I generally carry my clothes and other belongings with me or leave them in my hotel room during the day and seldom does anything disappear. I have always reasoned that if my purse or my bag was stolen it would return to the place from which it was taken, so even if I was robbed the crime would be easily solved since the thief was bound to be found near the scene of the crime again and again, day after day.

Now, however, I felt utterly lost without my bag. I wandered up and down the quayside, searching the area around the scene, even though I had seen the thief making off with my bag. From there I continued in the direction in which the thief had gone, checking in doorways and trash cans in nearby streets, but my bag was nowhere to be found and in the end there was nothing to do but to go back to my hotel. First, though, to be on the safe side, I went back to the restaurant on the promenade and asked if anyone had seen the thief or my bag, but no one there could aid me in my search.

I found no trace of my bag on the way back to my hotel either and there was nothing for it but to wait and see whether it would come back to me. The sensible thing seemed to be to get on with the day and go back to the spot where it had happened later.

At reception I told the staff that my bag had been stolen and since there might be a receipt from the hotel in it I asked them to keep an eye out for a bag or possibly a purse that looked like mine being handed in. They suggested that I report the theft to the police.

I found it hard to sleep last night. First I had trouble getting to sleep and when I finally did drop off I woke up every so often, and each time I woke I got up and searched my room for returned bags. But my bag did not return. It was not sitting next to my bed when I woke up after eventually getting two whole hours' sleep, nor did it turn up in the course of the afternoon. It was not handed in at reception and it was not sitting waiting for me out on the street or in any of the other places I then set out to search: the hotel trash cans, the cloakroom behind reception and the toilets next to the breakfast room.

This morning I made my first round of the streets and as the time of the bag theft approached I took another walk around those same streets. Whenever I saw someone wearing a home team scarf or hat and whenever I spotted someone wearing sweatpants or a hoodie, I would edge closer and take another look, but none of them bore any resemblance to the bicycling bag thief and I saw no bike that might have belonged to him. I went into several cafés and pizzerias, but nowhere did I see anyone who looked like my thief.

Later I went back to the restaurant on the promenade and this time I ordered a cup of coffee, but still I saw no one nearby who resembled the bag thief, in fact I saw no one wearing a scarf or sweatpants and not a bicyclist in sight. At around the same time as yesterday I got up and made my way along the promenade again, now with all my senses on high alert, but still found not a single clue to follow. In the end I gave up and sat down on a bench overlooking the river. Nothing happened and I decided to walk back the same way.

This turned out to be a good decision because suddenly, as I was passing the tables at the restaurant, I spied my bag, next to a table a little further away from the spot where I had been sitting. It was propped against a flower planter, as if I had actually forgotten it myself when I left. I rushed over to pick it up and frantically asked the waiter who emerged from the restaurant at that moment with a lunch order if he had seen anyone leaving the bag. I tried to explain that it had been stolen and asked whether he had seen a man on a bike, but he hadn't seen anything, and a Japanese couple who were sitting waiting for their food could say only that they had seen someone with a bag, but they apparently thought that had been me. Which was, of course, true, because I had just retrieved it, but I don't think that's what they meant.

To avoid complicating the situation any further I quickly thanked them all and went on my way with my bag before anyone had time to wonder. I looked around, but there was nothing out of the ordinary to be seen so I hurried back to the hotel.

As soon as I got to my room I opened my bag. Fortunately, both my purse and my credit card were still there, together with most of the things I had not left behind in my hotel room. I shook the contents of the bag out onto the floor only to find some other things which I had forgotten were in it, but which also seemed to be unscathed. The Roman sestertius, my pen from the Salon Lumières, a bag containing eight caramels, one woolen sock whose partner I had lost long ago and which must have lain at the bottom of the bag since the spring, and an old tube of dried-up mascara.

In one of the front pockets I found the memory stick which I had bought in Copenhagen, covered in crumbs and fluff from the bag. In another pocket was the flashlight I had found in my mother's broom closet. Also there was my passport, but the cash in my purse, about a thousand euros, had been taken. My seasons book, too, was gone, as were the papers and money that had been tucked in at the back of the book.

I don't know what has happened. It's hard to find a coherent explanation, but I assume that the thief took the money and held onto my seasons book, possibly because he thought it might contain valuable information. I suppose it must have looked strange with all those details about seasons, all those addresses and names of companies and rail connections and printouts of temperature graphs and whatnot, and the presence of so much cash might lead someone to imagine that there was money to be made from these mysterious jottings. But that doesn't explain how my bag returned to the restaurant. Another explanation could be that my seasons book no longer has any meaning. The thief took the money, dumped the bag next to the flower planter and my seasons book has quite simply vanished overnight.

I find it odd but content myself with the thought that the seasons book and the cash simply don't matter any more. As if they don't belong to me and can simply vanish. But why a book containing almost six months' worth of notes should be less inclined to stay with me than a stray winter sock remains a mystery.

Relieved and slightly confused I repacked my bag. The main thing, I reasoned, was that I had my bag back. An explanation for the behavior of inanimate objects could wait.

Not long afterward I realized that my keys were also missing, both the key to the house in Clairon and the key to Room 16 at the Hôtel du Lison. I felt a brief pang of concern for Thomas, but he is not mentioned in my seasons book, nor is the address of our house written down anywhere. There is no mention of the Hôtel du Lison in it either and the hotel address is not given on the key, so it would be hard to find doors with locks those keys would fit. The folder containing my notes is lying on the table next to me, together with the notebook marked with all my days and a couple of books that I left there when I went out yesterday. It sets my mind at ease, because even though I no longer have my green, clothbound notebook, I still have all I need.

Nonetheless, my thoughts keep returning to, and endeavoring to figure out, how the thief could possibly hold on to his loot and what will happen to it if he gets rid of it? Did he take the cash, the keys and the seasons book and then dump the bag at the restaurant or did the bag return all by itself? And how could my seasons book vanish? Is it now redundant? A thing for which I no longer have any use? I don't know. I know that everything is surrounded by a gray zone, that this suspension of time is beyond my understanding. But I have my bag back. That much I do understand. The cash doesn't matter, I can always withdraw more from an ATM. And maybe the seasons book doesn't matter either. My seasons are gone, but do I need seasons?

Maybe the things I don't need will vanish. I think of the missing keys. Maybe this worries me. But there's nothing I can do about it. Maybe it is a sign that I shouldn't go back. I don't know. But I know that it is autumn, truth be told it is November. It is not September and it is not October. It is November. The eighteenth of November. A mild day in Düsseldorf, where the supporters of the home team and the visiting team are drinking beer together, where the visiting team is losing and the home team supporters are riding about on bikes, stealing bags. Maybe I should just go over to the enemy. Maybe I ought to just live with the world as it is and accept that there will never be an Oktoberfest, that there are no longer any festivals, no Christmas, no New Year, and that I will never again see winter or spring, no Easter, no summer. Only November and November.

In any case, I'm not in the mood for festivities. Or beer, or gatherings where people drink beer and toast each other and steal one another's bags.

#701

I have nothing against November, though. Not after having escaped from my season lie. Not the way November looks here: warm for the time of year, with sun in the middle of the afternoon, a soft breeze, and I don't need to travel in search of seasons. I have no urge to travel and there is nothing I wish for. My only thought is that I am about to leave my second year, or rather, that I am drifting around in a time where there are no years, because I know very well: I have had no seasons and I am not scouting for locations for a film. Seasons are not scenes and locations. And you cannot construct a year out of fragments of November. Of course you can't.

#709

Nevertheless, there is a glimmer of hope. That there is a way out of my November day. That constructing seasons has helped. That I have come closer to a proper year. That I will be able to exit the eighteenth of November when I reach the end of the year yet again. That my life in seasons can help me to find a way out.

I don't know why it's so difficult not to think in terms of years and I don't know why I keep trying to hold on to this microscopic hope. What I can ascertain is that hope does sometimes come calling. A rare guest and not always welcome. I have tried to construct a seasons machine. I have tried to jump-start the year. Haven't I done all I can to be allowed back into time?

#721

But I don't ever believe this for very long. I don't believe it's possible to jump-start a year. I don't think that I will move on to new November days, that I will be able to speed things up and run off along my November road: seventeenth, eighteenth, nineteenth, twentieth.

I think that I will go on waking up to the eighteenth of November. To a time without seasons. A time without days of the week or months, without holy days or holidays or feast days, without calendars or dates. It is chronic and there is nothing to be done about it. I roam the streets, I am in November, I have lost my seasons. Goodbye seasons. Hello November.

#733

And now the year has passed. A year of seasons, I think to myself, but they weren't seasons. They were wreckage, fished out of my stream of November days. You can't jump-start a year however closely you follow the meteorologists' graphs and calculations and you can't construct a year out of fragments of November. It cannot be done. I try not to think about years. It isn't easy, but now I will think about days. Mild November days that come around again and again. And morning comes, and evening comes, and night comes and morning comes again. Same day.

Two years in the eighteenth of November. 733 days, and tomorrow 734, and the day after tomorrow 735. For how long? Till I die? But I am not dead. It is November. I am in Düsseldorf. Why am I here?

#738

I am here because of a small ridge of high pressure a little to the east of the city. It is the weather that has brought me here. I am here because it is not raining. Because it is not snowing. It is a November day, but it doesn't feel like autumn. It is just a day. Warm enough for me not to long for summer. Without rain, without the sharpness of winter. A mild breeze blows through the streets and at around three o'clock there is sunshine, but it is not winter sunshine, it is not the slender rays of spring or blazing summer sun, just sunshine.

I have found a place that doesn't make me think of Clairon-sous-Bois in the rain or Thomas without an umbrella. A place that doesn't make me long for the winters in old Selter's garden, with rime frost and a thin layer of snow. That doesn't send me wandering around shops, looking for signs of spring. I have found a place that doesn't make me think of Thomas carrying his summer body up creaking stairs. And down.

I am staying in a hotel room on a day without seasons. The afternoon is warm and I can see yellow leaves on the occasional branch when I sit on a bench in the park and gaze up into the trees. It is a day that does not speak of summers gone or winters to come. My November day is warm, endless and golden. What do I want with seasons when I have come to a halt in a warm and golden eternity? A gentle repetition. What more can one ask for?

#741

And now I have found an empty apartment on Wiesenweg. It used to house an architect's studio, but the architect moved out and it has been converted to living accommodation. The windows onto the street are frosted and no one can see in. On the poster taped to one of the frosted windows it said that the apartment was unfurnished, but that the former owner had left a bed and there are two chairs and a table in the kitchen. I don't need much more. One chair would have been enough, but I didn't tell the real estate agent that.

I had walked past the poster in the window a couple of times before it dawned on me that this was where I would stay, not in a room filled with the sound of a human being, not in a gray house smelling faintly of mold, not in the hotels and houses of changing seasons.

After procuring yet another phone I called the number given at the bottom of the poster in the frosted window. It turned out that the owner of the apartment actually lived on the top floor of the same building and I managed to persuade her to show me around it straight away. First she told me that she was just on her way out, but that she could see me later in the afternoon, or the following morning. I persisted, explaining that I was in the neighborhood. I would not take up much of her time, but I urgently needed to find an apartment. It would only take me five minutes to get hold of the money for a deposit and I could move in immediately. I added the part about the five minutes because it would seem odd for someone to be walking around with enough money in their bag to pay for an apartment they had just happened to stumble upon. After a short pause the owner agreed and five minutes later I pressed the buzzer on the intercom for the apartment on the fifth floor.

Shortly afterward I heard the echo of footsteps coming down the stairs and a moment later the main door was opened by the owner of the apartment, an elderly woman whose gray hair went better with the voice on the phone than with the brisk step on the stairs, which sounded more like that of a busy young woman who had more to do than rent out an apartment to a chance passerby.

My new landlady greeted me politely, albeit with some bemusement, probably at my urgency, but she showed me around the apartment while I introduced myself and told her a story about how I had come to Düsseldorf from Brussels for a job interview and how the job was mine if I could start right away. I would like to move into the apartment at once if that was possible, I said, and would be happy to pay a deposit and the first month's rent up front.

In the end she agreed to take care of the formalities there and then. We went up to the fourth floor, where I paid my deposit in cash. I presented my passport and she printed out a contract, which I duly signed. Twenty minutes after getting there I was handed the keys to my new home. I followed my landlady back down the stairs and let myself in to my apartment. My landlady gave me a friendly smile, waved and hurried off to find her car, which she had had to park a couple of streets away the previous evening because all the spaces close by had been taken and now she wasn't quite sure where she had left it.

I think I began to feel at home even before she had reached her car. I have grown used to these lightning strikes. I have grown used to the idea that nothing can be put off till tomorrow, that everything has to happen instantly and that, in my few encounters with other people, I always have to convince them that everything needs to be done that very minute, I can't come back the next day, it has to be here and now, because tomorrow is today, although I don't usually tell them that.

After saying goodbye to my landlady, I set my bag down in my new apartment, took a look around and then opened the door to the backyard, where there is a medlar tree with ripe fruit on it. It stands there in all its shades of orange and brown. They are the shades of autumn, but I don't think about that. All I think is: *medlar tree.*

#754

I don't know how one can grow used to a situation like this, but that's what is happening. Perhaps it is the case that you can accept a lot as long as you are spared most of life's worries. If you are not in danger. If it is a life with no drama, with no poverty or disease or natural disasters. I am safe, I have nothing to fear, none of the things one has learned to fear: the calamities and catastrophes of real life—loss, betrayal and crime.

My disasters are little ones and my accidents are fleeting: a minor burn, a twisted ankle, a car crash averted by a braking system. The greatest crime I have experienced is the theft of my bag, a crime perpetrated by a soccer fan on a rattly bike. The only things I have lost, apart from the passage of time, are a bundle of euros, an olive-green clothbound notebook and two sets of keys. I have what I need. I don't starve. I can buy whatever I want. I can go back to Thomas and slip into his pattern. He is still alive. I am sure that he is still there, in his house in Clairon. In his pattern. I have suffered no loss, I have not been betrayed, rejected, forsaken. Nothing has happened that one might fear. Nothing fearful.

#761

In the afternoon, when the sun is out, I can take one of my chairs out into the backyard and sit there in the sunshine. There is not much here to remind me of my life in Clairon-sous-Bois, nor is there much to remind me of my attempts to construct seasons. I don't have to model my every step after those of a person in a house and I don't have to follow any rhythm other than my own. All I have to do is to stay out of sight when my landlady goes out or comes back, because she has long since forgotten that I am here. She goes out for the first time in the midmorning and returns three hours later. She goes out for the second time in the afternoon when I am sitting in the backyard, but she is back in her apartment on the fifth floor just after five. Her husband leaves early in the morning and gets back a little before six. When they are at home I am free to switch on lamps if I want to because from their fifth-floor apartment they cannot see light in my windows. The other apartments in the building are rented, but their tenants are out for most of the day and I don't hear them much. Occasionally I hear footsteps on the stairs, but generally I only hear cars and trams going by on the streets outside. The sounds on the street seem to me to die down while the game is on because I can hear the faint whisper of the leaves on the medlar tree, a sound which I cannot hear in the morning, although that could be because the wind picks up a little in the afternoon. At night this sound is clearer, not because the wind gets stronger but because the street sounds are fainter. The trams have stopped running, there aren't many cars on the road and the sound of the tree is no longer a whisper, but the quiet rustle of yellow, almost dry leaves. If I go out into the backyard at night the noise is more nuanced, a welter of sounds unfolds. Leaves against twigs, leaves against leaves, a medlar falling to earth. It lands with a little thud and rolls a short distance across the ground before it stops. It sounds as if the world is saying *danke* when the tree drops its fruit.

#763

I have seen signs of Christmas in the shops lately. They have been there all the time, of course, but I have been looking for January, February and March, I have been looking for Easter and spring and summer and August and September and have missed all the little signs of Christmas, but now Christmas is starting to come to the fore. I think of Thomas, of my parents, of my sister. I think of presents, but no presents will be bought and there will be no time for Bûche de Noël or Christmas pudding. There will be no time for turkey or roast potatoes. There will be no time for singing duets along with the fridge's mirthful sobs. There will be no months and seasons and festivals. There will be November and I want November, and even if I wished for a year that would begin to pass, I wouldn't know how to get there because I have lost my manual. Thanks, bicycling bag thief.

#775

There was no Christmas, of course, and there has been no New Year either. And even though I have counted my days I don't buy champagne and I am not looking for snow to fall on my streets. My New Year's morning with white light and a view of snow-covered roofs feels infinitely far away. My year feels like a journey I left behind long ago.

Here there is only a neutral, gentle November day, because my time is not a circle and it is not a line, it is not a wheel and it is not a river. It is a space, a room, a pool, a vessel, a container. It is a backyard with a medlar tree and autumn sunshine. Coffee and sunshine on a day in November. *Danke.*

#793

When I sit in my backyard I can tell that my time is a container. That is how it is. It is a day one can step into. Again and again. Not a stream which one can only dip into once. Time doesn't fly anywhere, it stays still, it is a vessel. Every day I lower my body into the eighteenth of November. I move around but nothing runs over the edge. Time is a space. Time is a room. Time is my backyard in afternoon sunshine, with the sound of cars, with trams in the distance. My day is a container filled with a mild breeze and sunshine every day around three. The night is a container with a medlar tree that rustles in the breeze, and the night says *danke* when the fruit falls.

#844

I have fallen into a rhythm. My mornings begin at Café Möller. I walk a few yards down Wiesenweg and the café is just around the corner on the right. My mornings are all alike. I go up a couple of steps and open the door. I hear the jangle of a bell. I go in and sit down at a table, always the same one, a window table with a view of the street. I arrive somewhere between 8:39 and 9:12, because if I get there a little earlier or a little later that table is occupied, in which case I move a little farther into the café, but I am usually there on time. I order tea, and the tea is kept in large metal canisters behind the counter. I can see eight large containers. I vary my orders and hope that I won't use up all their stock. Sometimes I order bread and cheese, or yogurt with fruit. Often I don't have anything to eat but just sit there, drinking tea by my window.

My afternoons are as alike as my mornings. At about three o'clock I carry a chair out to the backyard. I make a cup of coffee, fetch a book and sit down in the sunshine. It is warm enough for me to sit there for an hour or two.

It is only my late mornings that worry me. I get restless, I go around and around on myself. I think of the sounds in the house in Clairon-sous-Bois. I go for a walk in the park a couple of streets from here, I do some shopping or visit a nearby library, but I cannot relax until the afternoon sun breaks through and I carry my chair out into the backyard.

My evenings are short. I make some food or go across the street to a Greek restaurant, where I sit at a table in the corner, and where there are people who do nothing but be the same every single evening. I have got used to them: an old man who, after a brief wait, is joined by a woman, most probably his wife, a group of adults with one child in a white shirt who tries to talk like a grown-up and two men of roughly my own age who gaze adoringly at each other.

Sometimes I visit secondhand shops and pick up small essentials that I carry around with me in my bag. At night I place my bag at the foot of the bed. It usually takes a few nights for these things to become mine, for me to be able to leave them in the kitchen: knives and forks, a paring knife, a coffee grinder which

I had to buy three times before it would stay put. I bought an armchair, which I put in the empty sitting room and which I have slept in two nights in a row, but I don't need much and soon I have everything I need.

I often visit the shops just before closing time. I find grocery stores and delicatessens with food that will be thrown out at the end of the day, bakeries with bread that cannot be sold tomorrow. If time is a container then it can be emptied, and if I am not careful I will soon start to see traces of myself all over town: things being used up, empty shelves, the tracks of a plundering monster, a beast on the prowl, the bloody trail of a predator.

I don't want to be a monster. I walk a fine line, I tread carefully through the world, I leave as small a trail as I can. I try to get through the days without stepping too heavily. Stepping lightly. A monster playing at being a butterfly.

But I know that my mornings here at Café Möller will eventually leave a mark and that sooner or later my visits to the restaurant on Wiesenweg will have to stop. And yet I go back, because I feel at home in these places. I choose different drinks, I choose new dishes from the menu, I vary my orders and hope that the kitchen is well-stocked. I observe the people on the street outside, I observe the evening's guests and wonder what I would do if that were my son in the white shirt, if it were me who was so in love, if it were me coming to join my gray-haired husband and I feel that I am among friends. Friends of a sort, even though the feeling of fellowship I had experienced among soccer fans and puddles of beer is gone.

#862

I try to conceal it, but I know. I am a monster and I devour my world. There is no getting away from it. I can eat leftovers. I can go hungry all day, I can flit from place to place and leave the tiniest possible trace, I can spread my shopping, I can opt for the fullest tea canister at Café Möller, but these are all simply attempts to conceal the truth, to make the monster smaller. I know. At some point it will be over. Empty cans, empty pots. There's no hiding it. I am a very small monster in a gilded cage. A cage in the autumnal hues of the park, with the medlar's golden-brown leaves, the fruit's golden skin. I buy oranges the moment before they start to go moldy, I go around the shops just before closing time and the labels on the packages of cold meats or beef in orange marinade are stamped 18 November, that is the date I look for, I eat what I can find, all the food that will soon be garbage anyway, and I carry my shopping home, and evening comes and morning comes again, same golden day.

#877

Does it help that I chime in when I hear the night say *danke?* When my window is open onto the backyard and I hear a medlar drop? I feel I am lucky, because there could have been disasters and tragedies, disease and want. I lie in the morning gloom and think: *danke*, and if I can't sleep any more I get up.

I know. I get up in my gilded cage and right outside there is a world full of turmoil, a black square. This I know because mine is a gilded world. I open my door and fly out. No, I don't fly anywhere, I am trapped, I carry my gilded cage with me but I am not blind. I can see that there is another world around me and that my suspended day is a very minor misfortune that has befallen a monster in a gilded cage.

Does it help that I sprinkle a little gold around? There is a person sitting outside the supermarket, I give him a coin or a bill. I go into a shop and buy a bag of food for a little family that sits on the square in front of the station. They find cookies and sandwiches in the bag and the next day they are there again, with their sign, a plea for help. Today they received a little money and tomorrow they'll be back and I'll get them sandwiches from the station and then I'll go home and sit in my sunshine, then I'll wake again, a monster in a world of orange and gold.

A woman is standing under some scaffolding, looking confused. She doesn't know where she is, she stands there with the sun on her face and cannot go any further. Her hair is white, it shines, and she clutches one of the steel poles on the scaffolding. I give her my arm and help her out from the scaffolding, I find a chair for her at the nearest café, I order a glass of juice. After a little while she remembers the name of the nursing home she has just wandered off from. I escort her home and the next day she is there again. This time I follow her. She looks around herself in bewilderment, she starts walking, I follow, she walks toward the nursing home, she walks in the right direction, I keep my distance, she is almost home, and then I stop and let her go. I watch her grow smaller and smaller, she knows the way, she doesn't need me, and maybe she is already going further, out of the eighteenth, into the nineteenth. Maybe it is me who is lost, maybe they are all heading into the future, the nineteenth, the twentieth, maybe they have moved on and left me with their shadows, and there is only me, standing here watching them grow smaller and smaller: the man outside the supermarket, the little family in front of the station, my busy landlady, the stream of soccer fans, maybe they have all moved on while I am left here surrounded by ghosts, the husks of repetition, imprints of a day long since past, thinking that I can help, that my cage is gilded, that I can reach out.

I think of Thomas in the house, of a row of leeks that never grows any shorter. Maybe he has moved on without me, day by day, 877 days. My parents in their house, the quince bush in the garden. The quinces, gathered up long ago, and the bush that has gone on growing, it has been through a winter and spring with red flowers, then yellow fruit once more and yet another winter.

Have they run away from me? I don't know, but that is not how it feels: like a life among shadows. I let that thought lie. It is only that time has ground to a halt. I sit in the sunshine in the backyard, soon the sun will go behind the church tower, the sunshine will be blotted out, the air will turn cold and I will retreat indoors.

#889

The day before yesterday, during one of my restless mornings, I spent some hours clearing out my pockets and my bag. That is how small my daily chores have become. My circles are limited, my tasks microscopic.

In my bag I found receipts and household items which I am in the process of making my own. It has become a habit, I keep these items in my bag and I always have my bag with me. At night it sits at the foot of the bed, leaning up against the wall and every now and again, when I do a clear-out, I discover what has become attached to me. Not everything stays with me, some things are lost along the way, odd purchases that suddenly disappear. If they are things I feel that I cannot do without I will often buy them again, but some things simply go back to where they came from. It is a loose world and I have got used to that.

I gathered up the shopping lists and receipts and laid them in a heap on the kitchen countertop before throwing them into the garbage can. I took out socks and underwear that had been lying at the bottom of the bag, carried them into the bedroom and laid them in a little pile on the bed. I put a vegetable knife and a pair of scissors in the kitchen drawer together with a tea strainer from one of the side pockets and dropped two crumpled packs of sugar from a café into a cracked cup on the countertop.

I checked my jacket pockets and found a pen and the Roman sestertius, which I must have slipped in there after I got my bag back then more or less forgotten about. I put the sestertius in the cup along with the crumpled packs of sugar and there it lay while I cleared up the last few bits and pieces and got ready to go for a short walk through the streets.

A little later, when I came back into the kitchen, I had forgotten all about the coin and when my eye fell on it, it seemed strangely out of place, sitting there in a cracked cup along with a couple of sachets of sugar which I had only taken because they would have been thrown out otherwise.

I took the coin out of the cup and turned it this way and that. I looked at the head of Antoninus Pius and briefly traced the embossed image with my finger. I flipped the coin over and studied Annona with her grain measure and ears of corn. I ran a fingertip over the uneven edge, weighed the coin in the palm of my hand, dropped it onto the countertop and picked it up again: A tiny piece of the past, a leftover from my clear-out, no longer able to find a place in my world.

I looked around the kitchen but couldn't find anywhere to put the coin. I dropped it back into the cup and nudged it closer to the kitchen sink. I had the urge to get rid of it, to dispose of it. It had lost all significance, I told myself. It had been a part of my life from my very first eighteenth of November, it had been there on the counter in Philip Maurel's shop, it had been my gift to Thomas, a love gift, an object that never did find its way into his collection and even though it had gone missing the thought of it had lingered when I was in Clairon, as an unknown quantity, an unanswered question in the mystery of the fault in time. When I found it again, back in Philip and Marie's shop, it became a farewell gift, a prop in their withdrawal, a sudden rebuff, the cancellation of a friendship. But it didn't mean anything now. It was just a Roman coin, forgotten in a pocket and found again, an object which I had brought with me, now lying in a cup on a kitchen countertop, unplaceable and rather in the way.

That this was no ordinary coin was obvious. It was, of course, a historic object, an emblem from the past, a baton passed down through the centuries, a metallic witness to bygone ages or whatever. But no more than that. Interesting, perhaps, with its reliefs and its symbols, but not meaningful. Not any more. A matter of interest only to coin dealers and people with a feel for antiquity.

And yet, not a coin to be left lying in a cup next to the sink, I thought a little later when I tipped the coin out of the cup and tucked it into an unused pocket in my purse. I pushed the cup with its sugar packets back toward the kitchen sink before putting my purse in my bag, slipping on a pair of ankle boots and picking my bag up off the kitchen floor.

Now, though, it was the thought of walking around with the sestertius in my purse that bothered me. It didn't belong with the legal tender in there. I took it out again and put it back on the kitchen countertop where it then underwent a strange metamorphosis, one which I cannot quite explain, because obviously it was not the sestertius that changed as it lay there on the countertop, but that is how it felt.

I swithered. I went back to the bedroom, I separated the pile of clothes I had laid on the bed into smaller piles and transferred one of these to a shelf I had put up in the bedroom, but shortly afterward when I returned to the kitchen, I felt this growing awareness of the coin on the countertop. A coin that wants something of me, I thought, although coins don't, of course, lie around wanting anything of anyone.

It seemed a bit idiotic to me, but as the idiocy grew I also felt something else. It wasn't just that the sestertius acquired meaning. Although it did that too. But at that same moment I felt a void coming into being, I felt a loss, a slide, a shift. It was as if a space was opening up, very slowly, not a big space, or at least it didn't feel big, but I couldn't close it again. It didn't help to turn my attention elsewhere. The sestertius had induced a feeling of doubt, a lack, an ignorance, I don't know, all I know is that I felt empty and alone and somehow lacking, as if the sestertius had been lying there before me, filling itself with meaning, while the void inside me grew. It was almost as if, in some strange way, a part of me had slipped over into the coin, into a piece of ancient metal, leaving an open space.

I had the day ahead of me. I had no plans. I had time to think about my sestertius, about its transformation, about my need to imbue it with meaning and the strange sense of a void appearing inside me. I had time to stop and find my speculations idiotic and to ponder my attempts to ascribe significance to this metallic trifle, my projection of what-do-I-know onto a piece of metal.

And that is what I did. Sat down. Thought. Came up with explanations. Marveled at this odd process. How things acquire meaning. Not that there's anything strange in that. Or rather, there is something strange in that, of course. In fact if you think about it, it must be one of mankind's weirdest traits, but it is one of those peculiarities which we simply accept, this need to invest everyday objects—wedding rings, jewelry, as well as lucky coins, amulets, magic stones, relics, and sacred objects—with meaning.

I sat for a while pondering what it is that we invest in such things. What is it that happens? A lucky coin is picked up on the street, the ring is slipped on, the reliquary is brought out. We fill them with meaning, over them we pour some sort of precious metal that we have produced from a corner of our minds and there they stand, these things. Full of meaning. And there we stand, illuminated by their meaning.

But there was also something else, I thought, when I approached the coin again, wondering at the strange, tremulous void that had arisen. There was nothing golden or precious about the coin on the countertop. There was something irregular and dark about it that I could not quite comprehend. It was clear, however, that something had begun to shift as I stood there in the kitchen, the coin had started an engine, set something in motion and I had no choice but to go with it. It wasn't merely a case of a coin that had suddenly acquired meaning, nor was it mere curiosity or a sudden interest that led me to go back to it again and again as I went about the apartment, ready to go out but unable to tear my thoughts away from the sliver of metal on the kitchen countertop. There was more to it, or at least that is how it seemed to me.

When at long last I left the apartment, leaving the sestertius on the kitchen countertop, it was early afternoon. I felt uneasy. I walked along Wiesenweg then turned down towards the river, I strolled along the riverside, thinking about the Romans and their coins, about the Rhine, which had formed the Roman Empire's northern boundary and all at once I felt that I knew them, the Romans. That they had been with me for a long time. I don't know whether it was me who had been following them or the other way around, but it felt like an old acquaintanceship, one which the coin on my kitchen countertop had suddenly called to mind.

Little bits of knowledge came into my head as I walked. Books I had read, a school project from my teens, a couple of Philip Maurel's remarks regarding the coins in his display case. I remembered sketches of Roman buildings in a book I had purchased for T. & T. Selter and I recalled lots of facts I had gleaned on my way through the seasons, glimpses of a European past, ruins I had seen on my travels. I remembered museums I had visited on my autumn days while I was quietly idling. I had seen mosaic floors and columns, sculptures and implements, the pots of daily life and the oil lamps of the night, the remnants of clothing and jewelry, bowls and colored glass, and had regarded it all with a faint and inquisitive apathy which was now gone, giving way to a strange, tremulous void, a need to know that drew me along the riverbank as I tried to figure out why this subject had begun to interest me. History. The history of the coin. The history of the Romans.

I was struck by a feeling of discomfort, almost like toothache or a slight dizziness and I sat down on a stone wall and looked out across the river. I was taken aback. It was starting to dawn on me that history had already aroused my interest. Previously, if anyone had asked me if I was interested in history I would probably have replied in the affirmative. I would have felt that as an antiquarian bookseller you were bound to have some interest in history and with friends such as Philip Maurel you cannot avoid taking an interest in the Romans. But that would not have been true. My interest in the objects of the past has always been of another nature.

I thought of the coin I had left on the kitchen countertop, which is now lying here next to me, and I thought of the books I had

left at the Hôtel du Lison, back when I let myself be carried
along by the streams of people on the street. I thought of all
the book auctions and my rounds of the shelves in antiquarian
bookshops and the coins in Philip's chronologically arranged
glass cases and I realized that it had never been their history
that had attracted me. It was the objects themselves. It was the
feel of the paper and the indentations on the pages, it was the
type on the title pages, the balance between red and black. It
was an irregularity in the lettering, the uneven impress of type
worn down by the years. It was the saturation of the colors, the
intensity of the print. It was the lines of the illustrations, a detail
in the engraving, the contrast between a color field and the bare
paper. It was the smell and the sounds. It was the differences:
the slow *flick-flick* when you leaf through thick pages, the whisper of thin paper, a gilt edge and the split second's resistance as
the gilding leaves the fingertip, the little turn of the hand as the
thumb runs down over the corner of the block. It was the feel
of the binding, a frayed corner, a sharp edge. My relationship
with books has always lain in the eye and the hands and it was
this that had sometimes made me stop by one of the cabinets in
Philip's shop and take one of his coins into my hand. The feel of
the metal and that weight in my palm. The reliefs and the ridges
around the edge. The images of emperors and empresses, gods
and goddesses. The tiny objects on the reverse: ears of corn and
lighthouses, scales and owls, daggers and swords.

It wasn't the history of the objects themselves that attracted me,
it was everything that had dropped out of history. The objects
of history. In my world, history had not been anything except
the period that had produced them. A time line, perhaps, that
made it possible to arrange things in a clear sequence, but no

more than that. I had never been driven by a desire for insight into historical connections, I had never wanted to find explanations for the peculiarities of a period or information on people's daily lives, I had not been interested in wars or power struggles or political events, I had not been fascinated by the spirit of the times or the economic conditions.

T. & T. Selter was never interested in history, it seems to me now, but that's not true. Or at least it's only half-true because Thomas is interested in history. Thomas reads Jocelyn Miron, he reads of rises and falls. He wants to understand. He wants explanations, connections and historical insights.

But I had never been interested in history and when I think of the hunger for history that Philip and I had discussed a little ironically as we sat there at the counter in his shop, it strikes me that I had always found it odd. Something felt by other people. Our customers. Collectors. People with a need for the past. With a longing for past ages, a kind of nostalgia, a desire to form meaningful connections with events and people long gone.

And now I too have been smitten. A coin gone astray and suddenly I am seized by the urge to know more. About Annona and Antoninus. About the Romans and their boundaries. About gods and emperors, coins and the grain trade.

A ship sailed past me as I sat there gazing out across the water. The sun had come out and I got up and turned toward the city center. I felt uneasy but my unease could not be walked off. I bought some bread at a bakery I had never been to before. I went into a bookshop. At first I just browsed around, but then my eye was caught by a book with a black-and-white drawing on the front cover. It was a map of the boundaries of the Roman Empire. I had seen this map before, probably in a book or in a museum. I bought the book and put it in my bag. In another bookshop I found two more books and then I came by a supermarket, where I bought a salad in a plastic tub with a big yellow sticker on the lid saying that it would be thrown out at the end of the day.

Shortly afterward I walked back to Wiesenweg, where the sestertius was lying quietly next to a cracked cup. I took my books out of my bag and sat down at the little table in the kitchen.

Maybe it was simple: I was caught in time and there was the sestertius. Once it had been just metal, it had been molten, fluid, formless and then it had stopped at the moment that it was stamped with the images of Antoninus Pius and Annona, a modius, ears of corn and all. Stop. Fixed. *Chink*. Out onto the pile of newly minted coins. A frozen moment.

The Romans too had stopped. A long journey and then they could go no farther. They had reached their limit, they had advanced a little, then retreated, and then they stopped and built a wall and the empire ceased to expand. A moment's vacillation on the spot. Stop. Fixed. *Chink*.

And there I sat, in the eighteenth of November and unable to move on. *Chink*. Stopped. Same story. Was it so strange that this coin had aroused my interest? Not particularly. Was it so strange that the Romans' boundaries had piqued my curiosity? Not really. The coin. The Roman Empire. Tara. Stop. Fixed. *Chink*. We were two of a kind.

There was still a little sun in my backyard and I sat outside with my salad, in my gilded cage on the edge of the Roman Empire and now I am sitting here, at the table, which I have moved from the kitchen into the living room, with the coin lying next to me. I have put the books on the table along with my sestertius and I feel it all the time, this urge or hunger or whatever it is, that will not go away. I felt it when I was out in the backyard, sitting in the last of the sunshine before the sun went behind the church tower. I felt it when I was rearranging the furniture in the apartment and when I went to bed after having spent some hours reading my books. I felt it when I woke up yesterday morning and all day yesterday and I feel it now, when it is evening again and I have spent the day making small, random expeditions into the Roman world: I have a job to do, an objective. Something has been set in motion and there is nothing I can do but go along with it.

As soon as I got up this morning I went out. I skipped my breakfast at Café Möller and by the late morning I had been to the library and filled my bag with books which I took to a nearby café and promptly started to read. It didn't take me long, however, to realize that I would have to buy a computer, something which I had until then considered unnecessary. I had used libraries and hotel lobbies and I had my phone which, although it lost its connection with the outside world whenever it was not in use, could be activated if necessary, but that was no longer enough. I needed a stable internet connection and soon afterward I went out and bought a laptop which I brought back to the apartment with the books.

The next step was to gain access to the internet. When I had rented the apartment my landlady had informed me that the building had Wi-Fi, I just had to use a password. I hadn't been given this at the time, but I hadn't needed it then. I wasn't intending to hook up to any network because there was no one I had to get in touch with and nothing I needed to check.

Now, though, I did need the password and I immediately began to plan how to get hold of it. My first thought was that I would have to repeat my meeting with the owner of the apartment who would, of course, have forgotten that she had a tenant and would, therefore, be under the impression that the apartment was lying empty. I would have to make it look unoccupied, I would have to call the landlady, I would have to persist again, persuade again, go through the motions of renting again, all with the one difference: that this time I would have to make sure to get the Wi-Fi password then and there. But then it occurred to me that instead I could knock on the door of one of the other apartments in the building and introduce myself as the new tenant on the ground floor and ask whoever lived there for the password. Or maybe I could set up some sort of mobile hot spot, but then I remembered the envelope I had found on my doormat on the afternoon of the day when I had rented the apartment. I had popped it into my bag and a few days later, when I cleared out the bag, I had left the envelope in the kitchen. I had registered that it contained a key to the mailbox in the hall but since I wasn't expecting to receive any mail the envelope had lain on the kitchen countertop until I eventually put it in one of the kitchen cupboards. I retrieved the envelope, which had been propped up against a water glass at the back of the cupboard and sure enough: inside, along with the key for the mailbox, my considerate landlady had put a slip of paper with the Wi-Fi password on it. I keyed in the password and just like that I had access to everything I needed.

#903

It is a strange search. It kicks in as soon as I open my eyes: my eagerness, my drive, my peculiar thirst for knowledge. It carries me through the day, it sends me out of the apartment and sits me down at the living-room table. It is a search that cannot be stopped. My books lie open on the floor of the apartment. Sheets of paper lie scattered about, covered in notes and lists of things I am in the process of checking. I have brought back books, I have no bookshelves, but the floor will have to act as a bookshelf. I bought a lamp which I switch on when I realize that it is evening. I sit in my armchair with a book or two. Sometimes I fall asleep in the chair, but usually I make it to my bed, and as soon as morning comes it is there again, my eagerness, my unstoppable search.

It can be put on pause. I am sitting in the sunshine in the backyard. I am recharging. I take a pause in the sunshine, but not for long.

#927

It starts with a blank morning. A sudden awakening. I lift my laptop over onto my bed, I turn it on and my day begins. Every day the same thing happens: I key in my password only to discover that all the information I had found is gone, but that doesn't stop me. That is just how it is. I cannot save documents or files, I have no search history because everything disappears overnight. That is how I work. I wake up in the morning. I switch on and start up. I explore the world of the Romans, I find and collect, I let myself be led in random circles. I follow a whim, a question, a curiosity. I am led onward, I roam around, flashlight in hand, lighting up corners, I lift a curtain, I blow the dust off a sentence.

At some point during the morning I leave my bed and sit down at the table. I go out to pick up some essentials from the shops, I sit out in the afternoon sunshine and in the evening I withdraw to my armchair. I read or try to remember what the day has brought me. I go to bed late and the next morning it starts all over again.

Initially I was nervous. That first evening after I had bought my laptop I packed it all up very carefully and laid it next to me on the bed. I woke up a couple of times during the night and checked that it was all still there and again in the morning there it all was: laptop, cables, books, the lot, but not the information I had unearthed. That was all gone, exactly as one would expect: searches, documents, articles, everything had disappeared and I had to key in the password again, but that didn't surprise me and it was not a problem. It was a freedom, I told myself as I tried unsuccessfully to refind an article I hadn't got around to reading. The eighteenth of November is a loose world, I know, it is impossible to get a firm grip on it. It contains phones that stop working, empty memory sticks, passwords that have to be keyed in again and again, searches that disappear overnight. Each morning everything is gone and the eighteenth of November wakes up fresh and unused again.

This is how I find my way into the Roman world. I have no aim and no plan. I don't need to delete my dead-ends, they delete themselves. I cannot get a firm grip. I have my memory, I note down titles, names and websites and leave the rest to oblivion.

That is how my days are spent. One after another. I wake up and roam around history. I can feel my brain growing. It grows through remembering and it grows through all the things I find. It grows through forgetting, it lets go, it leaves spaces to stand empty and the next day I search for new knowledge to fill the empty spaces.

Some nights I wake up and discover that my hand is lying on the cool surface of the computer. It makes me anxious. It feels as though something has disappeared, and I know that this is oblivion setting in, the digital memory is in the process of erasing itself. I sit up. I look around me, but my world is still there. I listen to the night and if I lie with the window open onto the backyard I can hear the medlar tree swaying in the breeze and possibly a single *danke* from a falling fruit. I hear the distant hum of traffic and if I don't fall asleep I can hear the first trams driving off in the morning gloom.

#956

What do you call a void that sets something in motion? What do you call an eagerness that cannot be ignored? What do you call a search that never stops? I give it names. An urge, a hunger, a longing, a desire, a drive. I call it interest, thirst for knowledge, I think hunger for history and yen for the past, but none of these is quite right. It is an open turmoil, an immeasurable void. I carry my chair out into the backyard. I listen to the medlar tree.

It stands there as if nothing has happened, peaceful in a very light breeze.

I want to know more. It is a machine, a thresher that has been set in motion. I want to press on. I load up my pack animals, I harness the horses, I want to forge ahead, I scan the terrain. I arm myself with patience, I search and I collect.

I am following the movements of the Romans. I follow them as they build roads through the countryside. I follow them to the borders that move with every year. I set out, we are expanding, we want to forge ahead. I set off after the army when it marches. I roam far and wide with the legions, with packs and weapons and herds of cattle or flocks of sheep. I am with them when they make camp or fight battles, when they steal and plunder and trade.

I follow their enemies and their allies. I observe them from a distance. I stand on a hilltop, I follow the battles and gather spoils from a battlefield. I borrow a horse, a chariot, bind sandals around my feet. I travel with elephants, a grueling trek, through snow, over mountains. I sit by the coast, almost invisible, when galley slaves row a warship into ambush behind a headland, I am with the one, then the other, then I go back and land on a friendly shore.

I want to press on, I want to plough and harvest, I want to gather in, I want to find, I want to make headway. A door has opened. There is a draft. The wind rushes through the room. The wind in the sails. A ship crossing the ocean. The cry of the mate. We are carrying a hold full of grain, a fleet of ships underway. I think of rats and creepy-crawlers, of pirates and storms. I climb the mast and spy harbors and lighthouses. I am there when the grain measurers measure the corn and the porters lug the sacks. I sail with the barges on the river and now I can hear the noise of the city. Buildings spring up from the ground. There are cranes and mixers and hoists. The cement that binds it all together.

I run alongside the aqueducts, lofty and ostentatious. I hear the water flowing over my head and I follow it as it streams into the cities, into cisterns and fountains and houses. I stand and look down into the Roman drains, the sewage pipes under the roads. I want to know more. How were they built and how did they come up with the idea? Ah, but they didn't come up with the idea. It was borrowed from the Etruscans, as were the aqueducts.

I see more cities rising up across the countryside, villas along the coast and more roads. I follow the supply lines, always fresh supplies being transported this way and that across the empire. There is salt from Asia Minor and olive oil from Hispania. Wine from the vineyards in the south, fruit syrup and fish sauce in large jars. And always grain from Egypt, from Sicily and Sardinia and everywhere along the North African coast, all supply grain, now it comes from the fields of Britain as well, and all the way from Moesia on the Black Sea grain is carried by sea to Rome.

I hear the mills grinding, turned by donkeys, water-powered, and then the slaves, always the slaves, and the bread, kneaded and shaped and baked in the bakehouse ovens. I see them kindle the fires with the wood from old vines and now I am walking through the vineyards, their small farms and their vast plantations, on which slaves harvest and plant and sow. One of the slaves sends me a look that stops me in my tracks. This hectic whirl of mine is monstrous. I am a monster who wants to know more. I plunder their history at two thousand years' remove and now I cannot get enough of it.

I am there when wild beasts arrive from remote parts of the empire: elephants, giraffes, crocodiles and tigers. I see the horses taking off at the racetrack, I see spectators flocking to gladiator games or comedies, but now I must be going, because now I am following the postal service, sealed letters sent from city to city, from camp to camp. I hear the sounds of horses and mules. I take the roads to Rome and to the coast and out to the boundaries of the empire, but then we have to head up into the mountains, to the mines, because the Romans need metal. There is tin to be transported, copper and lead to be collected. Silver and gold to be extracted. I see the Romans negotiating with contractors, and carriers while conquering new lands and distributing supplies. The mountains of Hispania are undermined, huge quantities of gold have been extracted, and now the tin mines are almost exhausted, so we have to get tin from Britain, the countryside is riddled with holes. We need volcanic ash from Puteoli for concrete. Harbors and amphitheaters and gymnasia and bathhouses shoot up all over the place. Concrete lasts forever, Rome is eternal and the empire knows no bounds.

All day I search and I find. I go into the houses, I sneak into bedrooms and kitchens. I sniff at the dishes being carried out of the kitchen and eat the leftovers, if there are any when the bowls return to the kitchen.

I don't make do with leftovers, though, I suss out the cook's secrets, the baker's techniques. I cook medlars in honey, I make a fruit sauce from stale grapes and bake bread, a *panis quadratus*: a round loaf leavened with sourdough then kneaded and shaped and the top segmented. I tie a string around the loaf because that was probably what they did and lift it into my oven.

I find plates and jars, I follow the potters and now the glass-blowers as well. They learned the casting of glass from the Greeks, but now glassmakers travel to the southern provinces, they bring back soda from the Natrun Valley and soon glass is being blown everywhere: a glass cup for a sestertius, a cheap one, but they are available in all colors and shapes, and they spread throughout the empire, which expands like a piece of glass being blown, a bowl, a vessel, a growing realm. We need wood for the ovens and I go with them into the trees and then the wood is felled and burned down to charcoal, which is trans-ported along the roads, and then it is evening again.

I race around all day, I get out of breath and by the evening I am tired of running after the Romans. I stop, I go to bed and fall asleep and before I know it the night is over and my search begins again.

#981

The days are all alike. I find maps of the cities and the streets. I collect sketches of houses and baths, theaters and harbors. I read accounts of battles and conquests, of power struggles, in-trigue and murder. I have lists of poisonous plants, of armies and legions, inventories of war spoils and catalogs of doctors' remedies for bladder infections, broken bones, arthritis. I find pictures of everyday implements, of clothes and jewelry and elaborately braided women's hairstyles.

I find calculations and measurements: the dimensions of the grain stores and the tonnage of the ships, the population statistics for cities and the size of legions. I find figures for wine production and olive harvests, estimates of grain consumption per Roman per day, the numbers for plague victims and for urban water consumption.

There is a choir of voices: the accounts of the historians, inscriptions from all corners of the empire, graffiti from the walls, letters and speeches and poetry, decrees and laws. I listen to reports from travelers of the past, the sense of awe when faced with an ancient Roman building, the wide-eyed wonder at a temple and the spine-tingling thrill induced by the smell of the steam from Vesuvius. I listen to the discussions of the archaeologists and the estimates of the economists, disagreements, mutterings in corners. I read about old surveys, established truths, fresh theories, the latest lab results and weird speculations.

There is no more room in my memory. It is full of Romans running around and shouting in the streets or writing to one another. It is full of treasure hunters and surveyors, building contractors and architects who run up and down through the centuries, discovering the remains of the Roman world. I encounter historians and philologists and archaeologists and now also oceanographers and archaeobotanists, geogeneticists, marine geographers and experts in archaeological chemistry.

I am starting to worry about all the things that disappear during the night and now I have bought a printer. I have paper and folders, I have procured shelves for my folders and the printer churns out page after page into my living room. Pictures and articles, summaries and sheets of scribbled notes. There are some spare ink cartridges lying next to the printer and in the evening I print out what I have found. I tidy up, file things away and go to bed, and before I know it the night is over.

#992

My days are simple, my head is full, my nights are quiet. I wake up in the morning and pull the laptop over onto the bed. I read books and take notes. I find illustrations, lectures, presentations, articles and films. During the day I sit at the table and as evening draws on I print out all my findings and take the whole lot to bed with me, both the printouts and the folders in which I have filed them. For the first few nights they lie next to my pillow when I am sleeping, but it is not long before they can lie on the chair beside the bed. So I do need two chairs, after all. One for sitting on and one for remembering.

#1021

I have discovered something alarming. Or at least, it's not a big discovery, but I do now find it alarming: everything in the Roman world is a container.

There are containers in the world. Of course there are. That's not what scares me. I have fallen into one, into time's container. It's not that either. But everything the Romans touch becomes a container. It's not only Annona with her modius. It's not only all that freshly blown glass, all those Roman cups and flacons and vases. It's not only amphoras and bowls, jars and pots and pitchers, household utensils of earthenware or wood. It's not only olive oil jars and cauldrons and wicker baskets, the constant stream of everyday containers that are filled and emptied as I run in and out of Roman houses and workshops. I examine their vessels, I turn them this way and that, I take the lid off a jar and when I turn it upside down I see that even that is a container. I put the lid back on, in a world full of containers.

I follow a woman who is passing through a gateway and there we are, in a courtyard with rooms running all the way around it and an opening in the roof. A house has become a container with light falling into the center and water flowing down into a pool when it rains. And the tenements in the poorer parts of town are containers. I visit them, I don't knock, I simply walk in and find that they are containers several storeys high with walls facing onto the street and apartments built around an open space, a garden, a shaft, an inner core into which the light can fall.

I walk around the Roman building sites, where one container after another is being built: not the low, wide semicircles and long, rectangular stadiums of before. Everything has higher and higher walls now, floor upon floor, walled arenas, on more and more storeys, completely circular amphitheaters, deeper and deeper containers, we always end up in a vessel, a can, a jar, and I stand at the bottom, looking up: at an opening. I can see the sky, I have fallen into the container and I cannot get out.

I view their harbors, larger and larger complexes, and the warehouses that form a crescent around the quay. Like a bowl the harbor endeavors to contain the sea. The ships drop anchor off a shore, in open sea, a bay scooped out by the waves. They sail in with all their supplies, whole fleets of ships, they make landfall, they reef the sails and glide all the way into the harbor bowl. A walled container.

I visit the thermae, where people immerse themselves in caldariums and frigidariums, one vessel after the other and I follow them through the different chambers, I immerse myself in their baths, I swim in their natatoriums, which are open to the sky, containers for swimming.

The temples too have become containers. I step into the Pantheon, light plays over the floor and high above is the dome with its eye toward heaven, an enormous oculus, and then the tombs, a mausoleum, open at the top, and then another, and another, scattered about the empire, containers to honor the dead.

And the cities, of course. Cities are containers, there's nothing new in that. For centuries cities have had walls and Rome outgrows its walls and before long a new one has to be built, bigger and higher. But the entire empire is now a container, the Roman container, and the walls define the empire. There are already borders to the south and now the walls run along the northern border. Even in Britain walls shoot up, first Hadrian's Wall, then the Antonine Wall a little further north, and then back again, and there the empire stops. Into the container goes Britain. Stop. *Chink*. The picture is complete.

That is what scares me. That everything has become a container. The boundless empire has been walled in, it is a bowl, a vessel, and the Romans get no further.

But what do they want with all those walls? Why do they stop now? Why don't they keep going? Why does the empire stop expanding, why do the armies stop conquering, the glassblowers stop inflating the empire, why have they tied a string around the bread to stop it from growing?

I want to know why. I search for answers but I have fallen into the Romans' container: I wake and search, I read and seek and when evening comes I go to bed. And before I know it the night is over.

#1041

My circles have grown bigger. I have visited museums and attended lectures. I make excursions into the countryside. I have been to see the aqueduct that conveyed Roman water to Cologne. I have been to Osnabrück and Kalkriese, where Quinctilius Varus lost thirty thousand men. I have visited *Limes Germanicus* and seen sections of the border fortifications. I set out in the early morning light, but I am always home by the end of the day. I sit back in my armchair, I read articles on the halting of the Roman expansion, I find new theories and studies and extensions to old explanations.

I read of Publius Quinctilius Varus, who let his legions advance through the Teutoburg Forest in scattered groups and was led into an ambush by the Cherusci chieftain, Arminius. Three legions—the 17th, the 18th and the 19th—were wiped out never to be reformed and I sit up a little in my chair. A gap has appeared in the sequence. I read about the Emperor Augustus who banged his head against a wall crying: *Quintili Vare, legiones redde*. Quinctilius Varus, give me back my legions. But Augustus doesn't get his legions back and the Roman Empire grinds to a halt, because Arminius proved more than a match for the Romans and then, suddenly, several centuries later he is known as Hermann and he is German. A folk hero, liberator of the Germanic people, king of the Teutoburg Forest. A monument is erected to commemorate his exploits, a Roman temple with no opening at the top, because instead, where the eye to heaven should be, stands Hermann.

But does a world power come to a halt because a general is lured into an ambush? A great empire that cannot defend itself against a loose collection of mutually feuding tribes riven by internal strife? There have always been border battles and lost legions. That has never prevented the Romans from expanding. I swither, seek other explanations. I read about alliances and trade, about battles and migrations, I hear of infighting, of disease and death, of epidemics and food shortages. I read of the exploitation of the countryside, depleted fields, moral decline, crumbling institutions. I think of monsters in containers, devouring their world.

One historian believes that Rome disintegrates from within, a colossus with feet of clay that has to build walls to conceal itself during the decaying process. Another dusts off the myth of Arminius and the redoubtable Germans, because while the Roman Empire is growing and flourishing the barbarians bide their time and grow strong. It is not a crumbling realm but a mighty empire defending itself against powerful barbarians, invading hordes. They are under pressure from the north, their expansion comes to a halt. An economist suggests that the Roman fortifications are not a defense but a threshold, an entryway. The Romans don't feel at all threatened. They have scented profit. The northern peoples want a share in Rome's trade and wealth and Rome builds walls to increase its control. Now the Romans can act, they can regulate the flow of people and tax everything that passes through. A border is a way of expanding and the realm carries on growing behind the walls, it swells and becomes as big and crisp as a freshly baked loaf from Pompeii. An archaeobotanist writes of the grain trade and shifts in climate, of newly discovered ovens and traces of pollen and now, suddenly, it is rye that has halted the Romans' advance. I hear of farming methods and growing conditions and the answer is clear: the Romans hit the rye-bread boundary. The northern terrain is too cold, the cultivation of wheat too difficult, the yield uncertain, only rye will grow there.

I sit in my armchair and read that the Romans came to a halt of their own accord. They could have expanded further, it would not have taken a great deal of Roman strength. They could have reformed the legions and conquered the whole of Germania, but they didn't, because there was nothing to conquer. No wheat—no Romans. Arminius might as well have saved his strength, the Romans would have stopped anyway, because it wasn't the Varian disaster, it wasn't the opportunity to levy taxes and impose duties and it wasn't the marauding barbarians or inner decay that brought the Romans to a halt. It was the smell of the bakery, because rye was *a very poor food useful only to stave off starvation,* according to Pliny the Elder. *Even when mixed with spelt to mitigate its bitter taste it is most unpleasant to the stomach,* he declares, and the physician Galen says of the black bread made from rye that it is malodorous and bad for the health.

Antoninus Pius has stopped and Annona stands there with her modius, but her container is empty because she has traveled far too far north. I get up from my chair, still with no explanation. I mean, did the Romans really come to a halt because rye gave Pliny the Elder a stomachache?

I know: I will not find any answers. The Roman Empire has become my mirror and now I have stepped into the mirror and cannot get out again. I have no idea why the Romans stopped expanding. Maybe they didn't want to go on. They stopped and built a wall. Because they didn't want to go any further. Maybe they simply wanted to live in a container with a view of sky and clouds.

#1053

But I will not be halted, now I want to move on. My circles grow bigger. I plan trips to Hadrian's Wall and the Antonine Wall. I consider traveling to other parts of the empire, but I sense a difference now, I read and search, or I sit by the water in the afternoon sunshine and watch the ships sailing along the Rhine before I go back to the apartment and sit in the backyard with my medlar tree.

I can feel a change in my search. I am no longer impatient. I feel a cool curiosity, as if my eagerness has been tempered, just a little, but enough for me to shiver slightly, sitting there in my backyard, and I go back inside, taking my chair with me.

#1064

It is a different kind of enthusiasm now. A cautious zeal. I have started attending university classes, usually in Düsseldorf, but sometimes I'll go to Cologne or another nearby town.

The first time I took the tram to the university I wasn't sure how to get there. I had to change trams a couple of times because I had gone the wrong way. I almost gave up, but now I often head over there around midmorning. I pack my bag with my computer, paper and pen and a dictionary. I sit with my fellow students on the tram, we make our way to the main entrance together, I go to lectures, and not only on the Romans: now I learn about the olive oil trade in Mycenae, Frankish agriculture, Greek harbor construction, ancient medicines or the Bronze Age collapse in the Near East. I have heard about prehistoric migrations, about newly discovered shipwrecks and diseases afflicting medieval wheat fields.

It is strange to be among the living after such a long time with dead Romans. I walk slowly, I stay in the background on the way into a lecture hall, stand in line at the coffee machine and roam the book-lined aisles in the library. I ask hesitant questions of my neighbors, in English and in halting German, and my fellow students answer me patiently, a lecturer explains a point, a librarian leads me along the bookshelves to find a book I wish to look at.

To begin with it was all new to me. I felt a little out of place among the students with their small laptop bags and knap-sacks, many of them unburdened by outerwear, looking exactly as if they were at home. I went around looking like a traveler, with my jacket over my arm and my big bag over my shoulder. I feel naked without my bag and even though I could leave it in my apartment, I don't.

After a while, though, I began to notice other people who didn't really seem to fit in: individuals with jackets and large shoulder bags who look slightly older than most of the students. I notice a hesitant movement, a searching glance and my own feeling of being an intruder has receded. I know my way around, I can find my way to lecture halls and classrooms almost as if I belong. I know the staff in the cafeteria the incidents of the day and the streams of people flowing along the corridors. At one lecture the lecturer tripped over a cable and now when I arrive I make a habit of swinging by that room and plugging that cable into another socket before carrying on to another lecture or another seminar.

I curb my curiosity. I proceed with caution among the living. I don't rummage through their bags or flick through their notes. I don't read their letters. I don't follow them into their houses or take baths in their bathrooms. I don't take photos of their jewelry or fiddle with the tip of a shoe. Such things are not done. One might perhaps bend down to pick up a dropped scarf or book, but one does not inspect their food or ask why they have tied a string around a loaf of bread.

I have mirrored the Romans but now I want to get out of my mirror. I see myself in shop windows when I go for a walk around town in the evening. I pass by the restaurant on Wiesenweg and see the diners at their tables. Sometimes I go in. I sit down among the living. I greet people discreetly but I don't ask any questions. I go back to my apartment, I print out a page or two, I go to bed and before I know it the night is over.

#1081

I saw my bicycling bag thief today. Or I think I did. Racing down Wiesenweg. Or heard him, because it was the sound of the bike that made me look up.

It was early afternoon, I was going off to do my shopping and had just stepped out onto the street when I heard this rattling sound, the noise of a bike in need of an overhaul, the clatter of an off-kilter mudguard or a rusty chain. The cyclist hurtled past, heading down Wiesenweg to the river. It took me a moment to place the sound and connect it with the figure on the bike, but the moment I realized where I knew that sound from I broke into a run down Wiesenweg. I ran as fast as I could, with my bag over my shoulder, past parked cars, with my eyes firmly fixed on the cyclist in the distance, but there was no way I was ever going to catch up with him and soon all I could see was a rapidly dwindling silhouette.

I stopped running, puffing and panting and suddenly unsure: had that really been my bicycling bag thief? I had seen no sign of the home team's colors, maybe I had been mistaken. Nonetheless, I kept going. I hurried down to the river and paced up and down the riverbank searching intently, but the cyclist was, of course, nowhere to be found.

Still out of breath, I sat down on a bench by the river, now suddenly filled with a sense of grief, of a loss, of something missing. At first it felt as though it was the thief's disappearance that had made me sad. The lost opportunity to talk to him. But what would I say to him? Why did you steal my bag? But I got it back long ago. I had it with me. That didn't matter now.

And then, all at once, I thought of the lost book, the one containing all my seasons. I felt like shouting: *Bicycling bag thief, give me back my seasons.* As if there was anything to be had from a book full of winter and spring and summer. I don't want my seasons back. What do I want with seasons that have to be constructed out of fragments of November?

I thought of Thomas, who'd asked me to go to Paris on my own, and Philip and Marie, who sent me off with a Roman coin in a mini shopping bag. I thought of my parents and of my promise to my mother: that I would find a way, that I would find my way by listening. I thought of the passengers on the trains, of my little thefts from their conversations, but I know: listening doesn't help.

After a little while I got up from the bench and started to walk back to the apartment. On the way I shopped at a small supermarket and when I came to the refrigerator section I added two cans of beer to my basket. I suddenly felt like going out to the stadium to see the match, but the minute I left the supermarket I lost my nerve, or interest, or whatever it was that I lost. I know the outcome. I know who wins and who loses and when the match was over there I would be. Standing in a container with a view of sky and clouds.

Shortly afterward, when I let myself into the apartment, the smell of stale air hit me in the face. There were bags of garbage in the hall. The kitchen table was littered with piles of plates and cups, its surface dotted with coffee rings. There were used tea bags and plastic containers with leftover bits of salad at the bottom. There were a couple of bowls encrusted with dried-up yogurt, there were books and papers and used printer cartridges strewn all over the place, and in the middle of it all lay the Roman sestertius.

I picked it up, turned it around, weighed it in my hand: a relic of my Roman search, abandoned among printer cartridges and unwashed cups, refuse left by Tara Selter, still alive and still trapped in the eighteenth of November.

I edged my way across the room and opened the door to my backyard with its medlar tree. I carried a chair out to the yard, took a cold beer with me and suddenly I couldn't help laughing, hesitantly at first, but soon so loudly that I was sure that I could be heard all over the backyard and on the balconies around me, but that was okay. A person is allowed to laugh if they find themselves at the bottom of a container with a view of the sky and know they will never learn how they ended up there.

#1106

My search is no longer a hunger, it is not a longing or an urge. I frequent lecture halls and cafeterias, museums and libraries, and when the day is over I go back to my place. I let myself in and I know: I will never find the explanations I seek. I will only find new questions and new answers.

I stroll around the town. I haven't seen any more of my bicycling bag thief. Once or twice I have run out into the street because I thought I heard a rattly bike, but there was no thief to be seen.

I listen to the wind and to the medlar tree in my backyard. I listen to the faint *tap-tap* of my laptop keyboard, because I am sitting here with the great pile of papers from my black cardboard folder, all the loose sheets of paper on which I have written in Clairon and Paris, in my seasons, in my gilded cage, in my Roman container.

I key the whole lot into my laptop in very small type and in the evening I print it all out. I listen to the printer, churning out sheet after sheet, my story, a story, someone's story, and I listen to my story while I am keying it in, because all of a sudden I am afraid of losing it all, afraid of theft and fire, of oblivion and disappearance, because there will be no one to remember and then there will be nothing but the leftovers: empty bowls encrusted with yogurt and plastic tubs containing bits of old salad.

#1132

I have counted the days and now I am thinking of quinces under the bush beside the garden path, because soon it will be Christmas. I could go back and tell the whole story again, this time with seasons and Romans. I could say that I haven't found a way out of the eighteenth of November. That all I have found are containers, one after another. That time is a space, a vessel, and that I have fallen into it.

But I'm not at all sure whether I want to escape from my container. Maybe I'll stay here. Maybe I'm like the Romans. Maybe I built it myself.

#1141

It is New Year again, but winter has not come. The weather is yellow and mild and I am sitting in the backyard on my chair, otherwise there is nothing to tell. It is quiet in my yard because no one is laughing. I try, but all that comes out is a very soft chuckle.

#1144

One should never say that there is nothing to tell. Or that no one is laughing. It is a quarter to nine. I am sitting in my seat by the window in Café Möller and I have far too much to tell and far too little time, because I have an appointment. I am meeting someone.

I got here early and have already ordered coffee. We arranged to meet at the table by the window at nine o'clock and there is something to tell. It is not about the Romans, or actually maybe it is, but it is also about a person with a bag. His name is Henry Dale, but I didn't know that. There was a lot more I didn't know. That he is trapped in a November day, for example. The eighteenth. That I am not alone.

I check the time. Soon I will know. If he has remembered our appointment. If he shows up.

No, now. I know now. I can see him from the window. He is walking toward Café Möller. It is Henry D., he is coming this way and there is more to tell, but not now, because he is approaching the door, he hasn't seen me, but the door opens, a bell jangles, and I see that it is him walking in.